MEMOIR FROM HELL

STEPHEN ROSS

BLACK PARROT BOOKS
San Diego, California

Black Parrot Books
blackparrotbooks@gmail.com

The Black Parrot Books name and logo are trademarks of Black Parrot Books.

Publisher's Note: This is a work of fiction. Names, characters, places, and incidents are a product of the author's imagination. Locales and public names are sometimes used for atmospheric purposes. Any resemblance to actual people, living or dead, or to businesses, companies, events, institutions, or locales is completely coincidental.

Book Layout ©2017 by BookDesignTemplates.com
Book Cover & Design © 2018 by Stephen Ross
Cover Design by QuarterbackTB at 99designs.com

Special discounts are available on quantity purchases by corporations, associations, and others. For details, contact the "Special Sales Department" at the address above.

2018 Black Parrot Books Paperback Edition.

ISBN 978-0-9970876-4-2 (eBook)
ISBN 978-0-9970876-3-5 (paperback)
Library of Congress Control Number: 2018930605

*To children everywhere, both young and old,
who have suffered the misdeeds of a parent.*

Eternally to Eliot and Alexandra.

A heartfelt thank you to my daughter, Alexandra, for her insight and suggestions that helped fine-tune this book into a better read.

Childhood should be carefree, playing in the sun; not living a nightmare in the darkness of the soul.

~ Dave Pelzer, *A Child Called "It"*

Child abuse casts a shadow the length of a lifetime.

~ Herbert Ward

Chapter One

~~~~~~~~~~~~~~~~~~~~~~~~~~~~~~~~~~

The stink of B.O. and shuffle of drunken, drugged-out feet almost always come before the hell to follow. I'd just turned four when the terror started. That's my first memory of the horror that run through my life—until I become a man and stopped it. Maybe it started before, and my screwball mind erased it. I don't know. But what I do know. I survived it. I made it. And I'm gonna tell you about it—all of it—even the parts that still make me wanna puke. That's why I'm talking to this tape machine: so you can understand what was, what is, and why what is—is.

My name's Jake Malloy. My momma used to call me Jakie when I was a little squirt. And my pa, well he hardly ever called me by my name. It was mostly "Hey, you!" or "Numbnuts!" or "Shithead!" or lots of times no name at all, just the pointing finger snapping at me to come. If he did use words with the twitching finger, it was always something like "Get your ass over here, shithead" or "Don't make me call your sorry ass again."

My pa shamed us all with such calling out for years: Momma, my little sister Dory, and me. He had some special ones he served up just for the girls like bitch, whore, slut, and a couple that I just can't speak out loud. I *will* tell you they're disgusting, terrible words for a female's sex parts. I always thought they was the worst and most awful of his nasty names. But the good news is, he don't do that no more. And I'll tell you why in a bit.

I guess things was pretty good at first. That's what Momma said. I'll have to take her word for it because I wasn't born until just after their first wedding anniversary. Momma's name was June, June Malloy. It was June Tompkins before she and Pa got hitched. But she ain't here no more. I'll get to that too. Like I said before, I don't remember things bad happening before I turned four. That's when my life turned to shit for the first time.

Pa never allowed us to watch TV, read books, or listen to the radio; and when the school give us stuff to study at home, he'd hide it. Me and Dory only learned whatever Momma could sneak in when Pa wasn't around. If he did catch her giving us studies . . . whooee . . . you wouldn't of wanted to be around. I can tell you that.

When I was about five and Dory was near three, we was setting on the bed with Momma while she read to us from a book some lady give her. Pa had took off, so we figured we could sneak a read. But he come back without us hearing him and opened the door. I'll never forget it. He drug Momma out by her hair, and yelled, "God Damn it, woman! How many times do I got to tell you there's to be no books in this house?"

Me and Dory was pressed up tight together, our eyes pinched half shut, hoping he wouldn't come after us. Then I seen him hit Momma hard, right in the face. She let out a cry, and in a shaky voice said, "I'm sorry. It won't happen again. I was just trying to read them a story."

When Momma's face turned around so I could see it, blood was coming out her nose and dripping all over the new blouse Grandma give her. I was so scared, and Dory was shaking as she pushed up against me. I'd seen Pa be bad to Momma lots of times before, but I never seen her bleed, until then. That's the first time I remember feeling hate.

That all happened lots of years ago. I'm twenty-three now. I got diagnosed with PTSD—that's some kind of post trauma something or other—and have been seeing a shrink for a long time. I can tell you it's helping, that and the drugs. But I still got a terrible fear of being around people, especially girls my age. I know I gotta get over it if I'm ever gonna get a girlfriend. Doc Samuelson—he's my doctor—is why I'm recording my story. He said it might help me to deal with the bad things from the past, start being with people more, and move on. I tried putting this down on paper a few times before, but I got to shaking so bad that I had to stop. I hope talking to a machine works better. We'll see.

I take a pill for the depression. I think it's called Lexapro. I tried a bunch of others before, but the Lex, that's what I call it, has been doing the best so far. The doc says it helps get rid of sad thoughts. It seems to be working pretty good because the depression hasn't got me down for a long time. There was days after my pa's streak of terror stopped that I'd sit and stare out the window, feeling kind of numb, not really wanting to be around folks, and not wanting to get out of my chair. I even cut my arms a few times. I still get depressed, but not as bad as before, and I don't cut myself.

I've had trouble sleeping ever since I was four. I used to wake up lots in the night from terrible nightmares: gross things with a bunch of heads would chase me while swinging swords, and I couldn't run fast enough to get away. Sometimes it would be my pa's head on the thing, only his head would be five times bigger than usual. When it was my pa, he'd catch me, and I'd wake up screaming just before he run a knife across my throat.

Doc Samuelson give me a sleeping pill about the time I started on the Lex. It works real good. I get about six hours steady sleep every night. There's still a night on occasion when I wake up because I feel like I'm falling off a cliff, or I see the bad things my pa done to Momma and Dory, or I feel like something is peeling my skin off. But them times are pretty much gone. I guess most everybody has some nightmares.

The doc says I'm doing great and should be able to have a regular life someday: get married, have kids, and stop the pills. I hope he's right. It might be good to have a girlfriend and to talk with people like normal folks do. Today, I'm just glad to be alive. I got a decent place to live, a fridge full of food, and a job that pays. Maybe one day I *will* have a girlfriend, and not have such bad nerves when I go out.

Enough about me and them pills. I wanna tell you a little about Hellridge. Stuff about the town, and the things that took place before I turned four, I was either told or seen in the local paper.

Chapter Two

~~~~~~

Most of what I'm gonna tell you took place right here in Hellridge, South Dakota, where I lived 'til I was nine. It's a quiet town of three thousand five hundred thirty-two people. That's the number on the sign out on highway sixty-five that lets you know you're here. The number of folks in the whole county ain't more than nine thousand.

Kind of a weird name for a town, don't you think? Hellridge. It always seemed that way to me. When I got a bit older, and things was real bad at home, I just called it Hell.

What I know about the town pretty much all come from things my Uncle Hank told me when I was a kid. He was Momma's brother from Idaho. He didn't come to town much, but when he did, he stayed with Grandpa Earl and Grandma Thelma. He was full of stories, and I liked hearing 'em. I don't know what happened, but he stopped coming back, and I never seen him again.

Uncle Hank said Hellridge was built up next to the Náhkohe River about 1850 and was where fur trappers and Cheyenne Indians traded and got supplies. Momma told me *Náhkohe* is the Cheyenne word for bear, and there was lots of 'em around back then.

The town got its name from a ridge just north of the high school that stands a hundred foot above the river. Uncle Hank told me a Cheyenne girl and boy fell in love and wanted to get hitched, but their parents was against it. Instead of being apart, they walked to the top of the ridge one night, spoke their love for each other, and jumped to their deaths in the fast current. Their bodies was never found. The only thing that told what happened was a beaver skin pouch setting in the grass at the edge of the ridge. The girl had kept her best stuff in it and always carried it with her.

Several years after the kids died, a young brave was hunting on the ridge when his horse spooked, reared up, and took 'em both to their deaths in the cold water of the Náhkohe. Uncle Hank said for sure that story ain't made up because several members of the tribe seen it happen and passed it on from one family to another—right up to this day. There's a stone statue of the hunter and his horse in the middle of the town park next to where the high school band gives shows. It was put up by a local fella who liked the story. Folks say it was the pride of Hellridge for a lot of years. People driving through used to walk to see it when they stopped to pee, or get gas, or an ice cream. It ain't been well tended to for a long time. Now it's mostly a place for pigeons to poop.

The ridge proved its name again about fifteen years ago when the local drunk decided to end his hurt. He put a slug in his head while standing on top and watching the sun go down for the last time. I guess he was in-and-out of hospitals a lot after his wife and little girl was killed in a car crash just south of town. I heard talk about that one time when Momma took us to Steiner's Cafe.

Main Street runs through the middle of town and is part of highway sixty-five. Some street-namer thought hard about that one. I think the same fella was hired by the next town over because it's called Main Street there too.

The part of town where most of the stores are is seven square blocks, and there's a few businesses farther out on the highway. Folks around here are either farmers or have something to do with farming. There's two feed stores, a machine shop, an irrigation supply place, and a crop dusting outfit that runs out of a small—little propeller-type planes, only—airport two miles to the east of town.

Most of the people around here are white folks. One time I heard somebody call 'em WASPs. I'm not sure what that means, because I always thought wasps was a type of bee. Bob Thayer, my boss at work, told me they come from countries like Sweden, Denmark, and Germany before ending up in this country. There's a pretty big bunch of Indians in the county too. They're related to the ones who camped around here way back. There's a few black families who come here from the cities trying to make a better go of it in farm country. And one time there was two Vietnamese who stayed out on the old Osterman spread a few miles west of town. I heard they moved back to Nam to be with kin.

The folks in Hellridge definitely got religion. There's four big churches. I know I seen signs for Presbyterian, Catholic, Methodist, and Baptist. Bob said they're packed to the roof every Sunday. The Catholics go on Saturday night too. Bob's been pressing me to go with him, but I'm not ready for that yet.

I never went to church—Pa wouldn't allow it. He said that's where folks get the devil. I wanted to go because I seen boys my age going in one time when we was driving past. I remember looking at them churches out of the car window when I was a kid and thinking how big and pretty they was. I still wonder what it'd be like to be inside one, especially when everybody was singing. I guess I'd better stop talking and take Bob up on it. Not sure why I ain't done it. Must be them old voices from my pa running around in my head that's keeping me from going. Well . . . that . . . and I don't like being in crowds.

I hear somebody knocking at my door. It's probably Dorothy Cannon. She lives close-by and keeps her eye on me to make sure I'm doing OK. She knows about my past and says she worries about me. I wonder sometimes if she might like me a bit more than just a friend. But I ain't never done nothing to find out. She usually brings me a slice of cake or a cookie she just took from the oven. A real nice lady. Reminds me a lot of Momma: about the same size, hair color, and real pretty blue eyes that's made me look at her too long sometimes. I reckon that's a bit crazy since she's around the same age as Momma would have been—forty-two.

Hold on while I get the door. I'll tell you more about Momma and Pa and how they met.

Chapter Three

~~~~~~~~~~~~~~~~~~~~~~~~~~~~~~~~~~~~~~

I was right: it *was* Dorothy dropping by to say hi. She's the only person I spend time with other than my shrink and Bob from work. She don't ask me questions about what went on before. And she don't try to touch me or get too close. She knows I don't like people putting their hands on me.

The first time Dorothy come over, she stuck out her hand like most folks do when they're meeting somebody. She saw me pull back, and she put her hand down right away. Dorothy's good that way. She don't push me for nothin': just talks about normal stuff and lets me know she cares. I don't think she knows how much I like her. Without her, I don't got nobody close. There's Grandpa Elton, Grandma Pearl, my sister Dory, and Bob. But Grandpa and Grandma are in Florida and don't talk to me no more. Dory's stuck away in the mental hospital. And I don't see Bob outside of work.

It makes me real sad about Dory. I don't get to see much of her. She's about a hundred miles away, and with my work and no car, it ain't easy to get there. Besides, the last time I went for a visit she was setting in the day room staring out the window. I stood by her for a long time, but she didn't seem to know. I called her name, soft at first, then a little louder, but she didn't budge. When I put my hand on her shoulder, it was like she wasn't there. She never looked at me and didn't say nothing. I set talking to her for a couple hours, telling about Grandpa and Grandma's house, my work, and how much I miss her. She hummed some tune I didn't know for a minute or two, then fell silent again, and never made another peep. I finally give her cheek a kiss and left. I don't even remember the bus ride home. Her doctor says she may get better someday. But right now, I ain't so sure. I hope he's right.

Now, about my folks meeting. One night when Pa was gone, me and Momma and Dory was setting on the porch looking for shooting stars and listening to the crickets sing. Momma got all dreamy-like and started talking about when she first met Pa: how handsome he was, how smart, and how she fell in love with him the first time she seen him. Here's what she told us.

It was a warm September afternoon just after they started senior year at Hellridge High School. Momma was walking home from school with her best friend, Pauline Crable. They was passing the football field when a ball come sailing over the chain fence and hit Momma on her shoulder, making her drop her books. She stooped down to pick 'em up, while Pauline run after the football and pitched it back to the boy who threw it.

Momma stood up holding her books just as the best-looking guy she'd ever laid eyes on come up to the fence wearing a football shirt. She stared at him, froze in place, and no words would come out her mouth. She heard Pauline say, "Nice throw, Mister! You almost knocked my friend over."

Paul, that's my pa, stood there flipping the ball back and forth from one hand to the other, staring at Momma, with a grin spreading from one ear to the other. "I'm real sorry!" he said. "Are you OK? I guess my throw was a little off."

Momma couldn't speak. She stood there gawking at him. Pauline grabbed her by the elbow and got her walking toward home. Momma said she kept looking back at Paul while she walked, and he kept standing in the same spot smiling, watching *her*.

That was the first time they seen one another. My pa had come to town a couple weeks before school started from some place in New York. His pa—my granddad— lost his job clerking in a grocery back there and got another one here in Hellridge managing the Farmers Co-op Grain Elevator.

Momma said she had a hundred butterflies in her stomach and couldn't eat her supper. She only got part of her lessons done and didn't fall asleep until four o'clock in the morning. When her ma hollered at her to get up, she threw down breakfast and run the eight blocks to school. Bad news hit her like a fast-moving freight when she got to class: Paul Arnold Malloy was out sick.

Momma hightailed it to school the next two days, but no Paul. On Friday, the end of the second week of class, he was standing by the flagpole talking with his buddies. She wanted to say something but kept her eyes down as she run passed: too scared to look at him. Her head was in the clouds during the first two classes. When her second hour English was half done, the teacher asked her why she thought Jane Austen's books had hung on so long. Momma was thinking about what she was gonna say to Paul when she seen him again and couldn't remember who Jane Austen was.

After the shame of English class, Momma went to her locker to get her math book for third hour. And who do you think was getting paper and a pen out of the locker next to her? Paul. She flung her locker open and fumbled around for her book. Momma said everything was a blur as she tried to remember what it was she'd planned to say to him.

"Hey, aren't you the girl I almost knocked

out with a football?"

With her eyes still fixed on the stuff in her locker, she said, "I think so."

"You think so? How could you forget? I nailed you pretty good. I hope you're OK, and it didn't leave a bruise."

Momma looked at him and her knees went soft. "No. I'm fine. There isn't a bruise."

"I'm glad to hear that. I feel bad about it." Then holding out his hand, he said, "I'm Paul. Paul Malloy."

Momma took his hand and stared at his face but didn't say nothing.

Pa finally said, "And you are?"

"Oh . . . sorry . . . June. June Tompkins."

"Nice to meet you June Tompkins. Hey, if you feel like it, how about meeting after the game tonight. We can grab a burger or something. I'm always starved after a game, and I'd like to make up for hitting you."

"Uh . . . yeah . . . sure. That'd be great."

"Super! I'll meet you at the south end of the bleachers. Give me a few to shower and change.

"OK, I'll see you there."

Momma headed off to her next class. She couldn't remember how she got there but thinks she might of floated.

The first date musta gone pretty good because they was going steady right after and got hitched the next July: one month after they was done with school. Both was eighteen.

Chapter Four

~~~~~~

Mamma said her Uncle Randy had his old Dodge pickup waiting for her and Pa outside the church after the wedding. People scribbled NEWLYWEDS and GOOD LUCK TONIGHT with shave cream on the rear window behind the gun rack. Somebody drew a picture on the windshield of people having sex—right in front of where Momma was setting. Uncle Randy said they made quite a racket driving away with all the beer cans tied to the trailer hitch.

Momma told me they drove a hundred-fifty miles so they could see Badlands National Park and Mount Rushmore. They slept in a fancy motel right outside the park. Before heading back home the next morning, they drove to the Pine Ridge Indian Reservation because Pa wanted to see the place where the Wounded Knee killing happened. That's a pretty strange thing to drive out of your way to see on your honeymoon.

I seen in the paper that reservation is one of the poorest places in the whole country. I heard Momma tell somebody that when Pa's buddy asked him if he went there to help out, he laughed and said,

"Hell no. I just wanted to see where all them Injuns was killed." That should give you a pretty good idea about my pa. Looking back, it should have been a sign for Momma to pack up and get out. But it wasn't, and they moved into a forty foot, single-wide trailer parked next to the shed at the back of Grandpa Earl and Grandma Thelma's place. They was Momma's mom and dad.

Grandpa Elton, he's Pa's dad, told me he got Pa a job as night watchman at the Farmer's Co-op Grain Elevator he managed. The pay wasn't much, but at least it was a start. Momma waitressed five shifts a week at Steiner's Cafe in downtown. Between 'em, and because they didn't have to pay no rent, they was able to make a go of it—not much of a go, but a go. Pa's shift started at ten o'clock at night, and he got off at six o'clock the next morning, every Sunday through Thursday. Momma worked from six o'clock in the morning to two o'clock in the afternoon every Monday through Friday. Momma slept while Pa worked, and he slept while she was at the cafe.

They started a bowling team with a couple friends from high school not too long after getting hitched, and spent three nights during the week, and every Saturday night, rolling balls at the Melody Bowl. They musta been pretty good because they won the league their first year. That'd never been done before in Hellridge: leastways, not as far as anybody could remember.

On his nineteenth birthday, two months before they was hitched a full year, Momma surprised Pa with the news she was gonna have a kid. He didn't say nothing, just stared at her with a blank look, walked to the fridge, grabbed a beer, and sat at the kitchen table looking out the window, drinking. After a couple minutes, Momma sat down across from him and said, "Paul, aren't you going to say anything?"

Another minute passed in silence. Then he turned to Momma with a dead look to his eyes, took a long chug of beer, and said, "What in the God damn hell did you go and do that for?"

Momma's mouth fell open, tears formed up in her eyes, and she said, "I didn't do it. *We* did it. I thought you'd be happy. I thought that's what you wanted. A family." She looked at Pa as shivers of shock hit her in the gut and tiny pins stabbed her face. When Pa got up to get another beer, Momma run sobbing to the bedroom and stayed there the whole night, by herself. A fourteen pound, bright-wrapped box with a new Brunswick bowling ball inside was tossed in the trash behind Steiner's the next morning. Momma had saved up for six months for that ball. It tore her heart out to toss it.

After that, things started getting real bad—fast. Pa went to his job at the elevator the next night without saying a word to Momma. During his shift, his high school buddy Darryl Jensen showed up with a surprise for him. Darryl had just got it from his cousin that was visiting from the city and wanted Pa to try it. He said it was a birthday present. Well, the surprise was a little piece of tinfoil with a chunk of crank wrapped up in it.

Neither Pa nor Darryl had ever done nothing like that before: other than smoke weed and drink beer. But being young and stupid, they crushed it up with a hammer and sucked it up their noses. I remember them two talking about it out on the porch when I was about seven. They was laughing and saying how they got real jittery and then started beating the crap out of each other. When I asked Momma about it, she said Pa come home pretty banged up and didn't sleep all night. He stayed on the couch, staring at the ceiling and grinding his teeth.

Turns out, Pa was one of them folks that gets hooked on crank right out of the chute. By the time I come along, Pa had already lost his job at the elevator and was living off Momma, selling weed, and collecting welfare. He'd also been in jail a couple times: once for breaking a beer bottle over a guy's head at the Melody Bowl, and another time for knocking Momma around pretty bad.

She should've dumped his ass then. But she didn't. I think she stayed mostly because of me: and the hope he'd change so we could be a regular family. Well, that never happened.

Chapter Five

~~~~~~

The first real memory I have of my pa took place the summer I was four. I was walking down the sidewalk on my way home from playing with the neighbor's new puppy when I seen Pa standing by the street in front of grandpa and grandma's house. He was walking back and forth and looking up and down the street. A beat-up, old car come tearing by and screeched to a stop right by Pa. He walked up to it. The driver's window come down, and a scary-looking guy I never seen before stuck his head out and said, "Paulie." He had long, dirty hair, a ratty beard, and some kind of tattoo on the arm that was hanging out the window.

Pa didn't say nothing. He kept looking up and down the street as he stuck his hand in his pocket and pulled out some money. The guy in the car reached out, grabbed the money, and handed Pa something. I couldn't see what it was because Pa shoved it in his pocket.

I tried to sneak across the yard and into my grandma's house before Pa seen me, but he turned around as the car tore off and growled at me. "Where the hell you going ya little shit? You know you ain't supposed to be at the neighbors without telling me. Get your sorry ass in the house right now before I beat it."

Pa started coming at me, so I run to the house to find Momma. I made it in just before Pa got there, but Momma was at Grandma's helping her clean house. Pa slammed the door and whacked me on the back of my head so hard I seen stars. He pushed me to the kitchen table and told me to set my butt down. I did, and almost started crying. It hurt so bad where his skull ring caused my head to bleed. But I didn't cry. Pa would of beat me for sure if I had. He always said crying was for sissy boys and stupid girls.

It was hard to set there and not touch the bump that sprung up on my head. My lips was trembling, and I scrunched my eyes together to hold back tears. But one got away and slid down my cheek onto my pants. I was lucky. Pa was getting a beer out of the fridge, and I wiped the tear trail off before he turned around.

He stood there staring at me with a scowl on his face as he popped the top on the can. I looked down at my hands and didn't say nothing: too scared to move. He come to the table, set down across from me, and pulled a piece of crumpled up tinfoil from his pocket. The stink that hit my nose made me blink and tighten up my cheeks.

Pa hadn't took a shower in days, and he sweat a lot, especially after he put that powder up his nose.

After guzzling the last of his beer, Pa slammed the can down on the table. It made me jump. He let out a laugh and said, "What's wrong ya little pussy? Afraid of a little noise?" I didn't say nothing and kept looking down at my hands.

The tinfoil set on the table across from me. Pa unfolded it, and I seen what looked like some white-colored rocks. He took a spoon out of the drawer and started to smash 'em. They turned into powder, and he said, "Hello, baby. Come to daddy." I looked around as best I could without moving my head, but I didn't see Dory, Momma, or no other lady. I wondered who he was talking to. There wasn't nobody in the trailer but me and him.

Pa got up, went to the trash can, and picked out a plastic straw. He pulled out the pocket knife he always carried and cut off a piece of the straw. He used the spoon to make a little line of powder. Then he bent over, put the straw up his nose, and took a big sniff. The line disappeared. Pa jerked back in the chair, threw his head up, and let out a loud, "Whoooeee."

He set there not moving. I looked up a bit so I could see him. His eyes was closed. I can still see his face. His cheeks was sunk in, and his hair was long and dirty. There was reddish-brown spots on his face and neck and dark circles around his eyes. He looked dead. I raised my head to see better. All of a sudden his eyes flew open, and he give me the scariest face I ever seen. His fists slammed down on the table and he yelled, "What the hell are you looking at you little turd? You like what you see, huh? You want some of that shit too? Is that it, you little bastard?"

My head jerked down, but it was too late. Pa jumped up and come around the table at me. He grabbed my hair, pulled my head back, and reached for the spoon. He jammed the spoon under my nose and said, "Here you go smart ass. Suck this up. It'll make a man outta ya."

I tried to turn my head away, but he yanked it back and pushed the spoon deep into my lip. "Now sniff it up." I didn't breathe or move. He squeezed my hair hard, and I could feel some come out. It hurt bad. "I said sniff it, damn it! Do it now if you know what's good for you."

I give a little sniff, but not enough to get any powder. Pa pulled the spoon away and smacked me on the head. He put the powder back under my nose, and screamed, "You do it now, or I'll beat the crap out of you." I started to cry, and without even thinking, sucked up all the powder. My face got hot, and it felt like lots of needles was sticking in my arms. Pa just laughed and said, "Good shit, ain't it?"

The shaking started in my hands, then moved all over my body. My eyes got blurry just before I threw up all over the rest of Pa's powder. The next thing I knew, my face was smashed down hard on the table, and I heard this beast-like roar come out of Pa. "God damn you. You fucking idiot. Do you know how much that shit costs? Huh? Do you?"

Blood was coming out my nose, but he made me walk to the sink for paper towels to wipe up the mess I made. As I dropped the last paper towel into the trash can, Pa give me a hard push from behind, and I went sprawling on the floor. He kicked my leg and said, "Get your sorry ass in your room, and don't come out 'til I tell you to."

I went to my room, set on my bed, and busted into silent crying. Tears mixed with blood and snot from my nose run down my face and onto my T-shirt.

I musta fell asleep because the next thing I remember Momma and Dory come in the trailer. I set up and peeked through the crack in the door. Momma and Dory stood froze, looking at Pa. He stared at 'em with a nasty, mean look. His nose was close to Momma's face. It was eerie quiet for a long time. Pa pulled back his fist and hit Momma hard in the face, knocking her off her feet and headfirst onto the floor. Momma let out a cry like when a dog gets beat. Dory stood looking down at her, too scared to move. I seen a puddle on the floor by Dory where she pissed herself.

Pa reached down, grabbed Momma by the hair, and yelled, "Where the hell you been? I ain't eaten because you wasn't here to make me nothing. Well, it's too late now, bitch. Get your ass in the back with your sissy-pants boy. You too, Dory." Then he dragged Momma into the bedroom. Me and Dory followed. Momma kept crying, "Paul! Stop! You're hurting me." But he kept on dragging her.

Pa spit on Momma in the bedroom and said, "Get your butt up on that bed and don't move." We set hugging each other as Pa walked out and slammed the door. Momma kept kissing me and Dory over and over while tears run down her face and onto our heads. We was shaking like leaves in a hard wind and holding onto Momma for dear life. She tried to make us feel better and said, "It's going to be OK. Your dad loves you and doesn't mean anything by this. He's just having some troubles right now and is upset. It'll get better. Promise."

When we started to quiet down, the door bust open, and Pa come in carrying a piece of rope. He pushed me and Dory on the floor and pulled Momma up to the top of the bed. He tied one end of the rope around her hands and the other end to the bed. He didn't say nothing and walked out banging the door closed. Me and Dory jumped on the bed and threw our arms and legs around Momma, holding her tight. I can still hear Dory crying, "Mommy! Mommy! Mommy!"

Pa smashed some bottles against the bedroom door. Then it got still. He musta took off. We fell asleep sometime in the night, because the next thing I knew, it was morning.

Chapter Six

~~~~~~~~~~~~~~~~~~~~~~~~~~~~~~~~

A barking dog snapped me awake. The sun was shining right in my eyes, so I put my hand up to block it. When I looked over at Momma, she was staring right at me with a worried look on her face. Her hands was tied to the bed, and Dory was tucked up tight against her, asleep, with one arm flung over Momma's chest.

A tear run down Momma's cheek, and she whispered, "I love you, Jakie. I love you so much. You know that, right?"

"I know Momma. I love you too." I reached up and put my hand on her cheek and said, "Are you OK, Momma?"

"Yes, I'm fine. You've been sleeping for a while. That's good. How do you feel?"

"I feel good. But Momma . . ."

"What is it, Jakie?"

"I'm scared. I don't want Pa hurting you no more."

"Aw, you don't have to worry about me. Your daddy won't do that again. Don't you worry."

"OK, Momma."

Then she looked at me real serious like and said, "I haven't heard anybody moving around out there. Stand up on the bed and see if your daddy's truck is here. Move slow and try not to make any noise."

I got up on my knees, grabbed hold of the bedpost to steady myself, and stood up. Pa's pickup wasn't parked where he always kept it. I pressed my cheek against the glass and looked all around from the back alley to the street. His truck wasn't nowhere in sight. "Momma, his truck ain't here."

"OK. Listen to me, Jakie. Listen careful. Open the door real slow and peek to see if your daddy's out there. If you don't see him, go to the drawer where we keep spoons and such and bring me the knife I use to cut up meat. You know. The one with the black handle."

I whispered, "OK, Momma."

"And Jakie, be very careful. That knife is sharp. I don't want you getting cut."

"I will, Momma."

My feet inched their way over the bed and touched the bare linoleum floor. I took one step, two steps, three steps. Then it happened. I stepped on the one loose spot in the floor, and a squeak roared out louder than I ever heard it before. I froze and looked quick at Momma. She give me a little smile, and in a soft voice said, "It's OK. Keep going."

I opened the door slow, just a crack, hoping it wouldn't squeak. I looked down the hall but didn't see him anywheres that was visible. I listened hard and didn't hear nothing other than the *drip drip drip* from the leaky bathroom faucet. I was so scared. My legs was shaking, and a shudder run through my guts. I thought for sure I was gonna throw up.

I crept into the hall, testing the floor for loose spots. I peeked in the bathroom but didn't see no sign of him. When I got near the kitchen, I could smell my puke in the trash can. There was flies buzzing round it that musta got in through the tear in the window screen. I didn't see my pa nowhere, so I went to the drawer and got the knife like Momma asked. I run back down the hall as soft as I could and showed Momma the knife. She smiled and said, "Good job, Jakie. Now be careful and cut the rope. Slide the sharp part of the blade back and forth on the piece between my hands. Keep the sharp edge turned up and away from my skin. Go slow so you don't stick yourself—or me."

I crawled up on the bed and done just what Momma said. I put the knife on the rope and started to cut. The rope was pretty thick, so it took me awhile to get all the way through. But it finally come apart, and Momma was free. She set up, pulled me and Dory into her chest, and squeezed us so hard it kind of hurt. But it was a good hurt, because I knew Momma loved us so much and would do whatever she could to protect us from Pa.

The joy we was feeling from Momma being free didn't last long. As soon as she let us go from her bear hug, we heard Pa's truck pull up and stop next to the trailer. Me and Dory looked up at Momma and almost started crying. Momma could see we was scared half to death, so she pulled us back close to her and rocked back and forth. She kissed both of us a bunch of times on our heads, and whispered, "Don't worry. It's going to be OK. I'm here. Nobody's going to hurt you."

We heard Pa walk up the steps, open the door, and come inside. We all froze. I don't even remember breathing. The fridge door opened, and we heard the sound of a can being popped. Then heavy footsteps come down the hall toward us. Momma squeezed us tighter to her, and Dory let out a little squeak, kind of like a rabbit that's been shot.

The bedroom door opened, and Pa stood there leaning against the frame. He stared at us with a dead look in his eyes. A shiver run through me, and I wondered what was coming next. Pa stepped into the room, flicked his thumb toward the door, and said, "Get out!"

The three of us jumped up and run out the door to Grandma's house. We stayed inside with the doors locked the whole day and night.

That's the end of my first recollection of Pa. But hold on, there's more—lots more.

Chapter Seven

~~~~~~~~~~~~~~~~~~~~~~~~~~~~~~~~~~~~~

Things was normal for a few days after Pa tied Momma to the bed. Not good, but normal for us. Pa didn't beat Momma or Dory that I know of, and he didn't hit me. That was the good part. But he still did lots of crank and would bust out into rages: yelling, shaking, and throwing stuff.

One time he threw a glass angel against the fridge and broke it into a hundred pieces. That hurt Momma bad because Grandma give it to her on her first communion. But she didn't say nothing for fear he'd start throwing *her* around. She got the broom out of the hall closet and swept it up. I was setting on the couch and seen her face when she dumped it in the trash. There was tears running down her cheeks.

I don't think Pa ever told Momma he was sorry for tying her up like he did. Probably because he wasn't. He didn't talk to any of us much. But when he did, it was always with an angry voice, and he almost never used our real names: just the nasty ones I told you about earlier.

Pa wasn't around much for months after he tied Momma. We never knew where he went or when he was coming back. So we was always kind of on edge and keeping our ears out for the sound of his truck. I heard Momma tell Grandma that she thought he was seeing a woman in the next town over. But Momma never crossed him about it for fear of getting beat. I think she was glad for the times he wasn't around, no matter what he was up to.

Lots of times when Pa come home I could smell something sweet in the air when he walked past me. I'm pretty sure it was la-dies' perfume, but I didn't know what it was at the time. Momma musta thought so too, because a few times after he passed by, I seen her working the air with her nose. Right away she'd look down and get a sad look on her face.

I remember the time Pa walked by me on his way out to who knows where, and the sweet air hit me. After he drove off, I asked Momma, "How come Pa sometimes smells like flowers?"

She said, "He probably brushed up against a lilac bush. You know, like the ones growing down the street by the mar-ket. Remember?"

"Yeah. I know what you mean. But that smell from Pa don't smell like lilacs to me."

Momma didn't say nothing. She kept drying the dishes, and we never talked about it again.

During the time Pa was gone so much, Grandma Thelma got books from the library and kept 'em at her house. Momma would read to me and Dory at Grandma's almost every day. One of my favorites was by some guy named Shel. I thought it was funny to have a name the same as what you call the outside of an egg. The book was about a tree that give stuff to a little boy. I couldn't figure out why the boy wanted the tree to give more than the apples it first give him. We hardly got apples, except at Grandma's. To sit on a tree branch and eat apples 'til you was stuffed sounded really good to me.

Another one of my favorite books was *Where The Wild Things Are.* It scared Dory at first because of all the monster pictures. But she got over it and started asking Momma to read it. I was older and could tell the monsters was friendly from their faces. But I did ask Momma, "Are there monsters like that for real?" Dory looked up at her real quick when I asked.

Momma said, "No. There are no real monsters like in the book. It's just a pretend story."

I was happy to hear that, and I seen a little smile come across Dory's mouth.

One day Momma asked, "How would you two like to start learning some numbers?"

I said, "I already know the numbers one to ten. Is there more?"

Momma let out a little laugh, one of the only times I remember her laughing, and said, "There are lots more numbers. And there's a lot of stuff you can do with them. Like, if you have one apple, and somebody gives you another one, you have two apples. That's called addition. One apple, plus one apple, equals two apples. Get it?"

"Yeah! I do. Can we learn some more?"

"Sure."

So Momma showed us how to add and take away numbers. I thought it was pretty cool. Dory started to get it too.

Momma warned us, "When your Pa is home, don't say anything about us reading and doing numbers. He won't like it. Promise?"

I said, "I promise, Momma." Dory shook her head up and down.

We almost got into trouble around the time we started learning how to take away numbers. Pa was home all strung out from snorting powder up his nose when Dory run up to Momma, and said, "Can we read about monsters?"

Momma dropped the box of cereal she was holding, and it spilled all over the floor. Pa's head jerked up, and he looked at Dory with hate on his face. Momma bent down to scoop up the cereal, and Pa growled, "What the hell did you say?"

The light went out of Dory's face. She put her arms around Momma's leg and squeezed tight. Momma covered quick and said, "She doesn't mean anything by it. I took her with me to the market the other day, and she heard some kids saying they'd read something about monsters. That's all." Then looking down at Dory, she said, "Right, honey?" Dory was froze. She didn't say or do nothing. She just clung to Momma.

Pa musta bought it, or the drugs made him forget, because he set back in the lounger and stared out the window.

The days when Pa was gone so much was the happiest time I remember about being a kid. But it didn't last long. Before I turned six, the shit come down again.

Chapter Eight

~~~~~~~~~~~~~~~~~~~~~~~~~~~~~~~~~~~

I remember the day I wish I could never remember. I get sick in my gut every time it comes to my mind. It's the day I come to know that Dory was being hurt bad—real bad. Hurt like no little girl should ever be hurt. It was the day when I first wished my pa was dead.

Big, fluffy clouds was rolling by overhead. The sun kept jumping out from behind a cloud, then hide, jump out, and hide again, over and over. It made the bedroom light up, go dark, then light up again: like a lamp being switched on and off.

It was a cool fall day, and I was lying in bed trying to see animals in the clouds. Everybody else was up. I heard Momma getting bowls out of the cupboard for cereal, and Dory was chattering about something. Pa slammed the bathroom door like he always done and shuffled down the hall. Dory went quiet, and Pa let out a big burp. He musta had his morning beers and a snort of the white powder. That's pretty much how he started every day.

I heard Momma say, "We're out of milk. I'm gonna run to the market. I'll be right back."

Pa said, "You better be. I'm hungry. And get me another six-pack of Bud."

Momma didn't say nothing. The door shut, and she walked across the deck and down the steps.

I stayed in bed with the blanket pulled up tight around my neck, but I didn't look for no more cloud animals. My ears was fixed on hearing where Pa was: hoping he wouldn't come to get me.

It was quiet for a bit. Then I heard a muffled squeal come from Dory. It kinda sounded like the noise some animals make when they been hurt. I crawled out of bed and started down the hall to see what she was doing.

I knew something wasn't right as soon as I got to the living room. Dory was leaning back into the couch, and Pa was knelt down on the floor in front of her. Her eyes was wide open and had the look of terror in 'em. I seen Pa's arm move forward a little, then back. He kept doing it over and over.

I musta made a sound because Pa whipped around and glared at me. That's when I seen what was going on. Dory's new pink dress was pulled up, and her panties was off. She started to bawl.

Pa had a shocked, crazy look in his eyes, and yelled, "What the hell you looking at, shit for brains?"

Fear froze me in place, and I looked down at the floor. Pa jumped up and come running over to me. The next thing I know, his big fist smashed into my face. I flew back about five feet and smacked my head on the kitchen counter. I musta blacked out because the next thing I remember is him holding me up by my T-shirt, shaking me, and screaming, "Don't you ever sneak up on me like that again. Got it?"

I was too dizzy and scared to talk, so he dropped me on the floor and dragged me by my hair over to the couch. Dory was lying on her side with her hands over her face—crying real hard. Pa slapped her legs and told her to shut the hell up. She quieted a bit but was still sobbing through her fingers.

Pa jerked me up by my arm and threw me on the couch next to Dory. It hurt real bad. Felt like my arm was tore off. Tears started coming to my eyes, but I didn't cry. I set there biting my teeth together, shaking, and staring at the clock on the stove. It kind of took me out of there and into someplace else. A better place.

He jerked Dory up by her arm and shoved her back against the couch. She screamed, so he smacked her upside the head to make her quiet down. She give out a yelp. But then she went silent. Her body was shaking so much that I could feel trembling through the couch.

Two bony hands shot out. One grabbed my face, and the other got Dory. Pa squeezed so hard that I felt my teeth cutting into my cheeks, and I tasted blood. He pulled our faces close to his, and said in a hollow, dead voice, "Don't you say nothing about this to no one. Get it?"

We was too scared to answer but kept looking in them sunken, yellow eyes.

His voice got low and raspy, and he said, "I said, do you get it?"

I swear, I thought the sound come from the devil himself. Although we couldn't say nothing because our faces was being pinched, we kind of bobbed our heads up and down a little to show we got it.

As soon as Pa let go of his grip, his finger shot up and pointed back and forth from my eyes to Dory's, and he growled, "You better get it. Because if you don't, I'm gonna hurt your Ma like she ain't never been hurt before."

We heard Momma coming up the deck steps. Pa give us one more death stare, shook his finger at us, and stood up as Momma come in the door with milk and beer. I could tell she knew something wasn't right. She looked over at us and stopped: her eyes moved from my Pa to Dory to me. Her face dropped, and a look of fear come back into her eyes. She musta knew what was going on because Dory's dress was still pulled up a bit, her panties was on the floor in front of the couch, and I had a big cherry around my eye.

Pa looked at her and said, "What are you gawking at? Give me a beer and get on that breakfast."

Momma walked to the kitchen and set the bag down without saying a word. She poured cereal and milk in the bowls, popped open a beer, took spoons out of the drawer, and handed each of us our breakfast. Then she hurried to the bathroom and shut the door. I heard quiet sobs coming from Momma as we ate our food in silence.

None of us ever talked about it again—until now.

Chapter Nine

~~~~~~~~~~~~~~~~~~~~~~~~~~~~~~~~~~~~~~~

A big change come to our lives the spring after I seen Pa messing with Dory. Grandpa Elton and Grandma Pearl moved away from Hellridge. Grandpa lost his job at the grain elevator, so they decided to try their luck in Florida. Some friend of his give him a lead on work down there and spending the winters in warm weather sounded pretty good for a change.

When they moved to Hellridge, Grandpa used the money from the house they sold in New York to buy an old shack on a couple acres two miles west of town. It set way back off the county road and had lots of trees around it. You couldn't see it from the road. There was a run-down tool shed behind the house, a dried-up well, and a root cellar dug into the side of a hill at the very back of the property. The nearest neighbor was half a mile away.

As luck would have it for my pa, Grandpa decided not to sell the place in case Florida didn't pan out and they wanted to move back. He told Pa we could move in and get out of the trailer: it would be good for us to have more room. And there'd be no rent if Pa kept the place up. That was a joke because there was nothing to keep up except maybe mowing the weeds. It had fell to ruin a long time ago.

The day Grandpa and Grandma moved out, Pa threw our stuff in his truck and moved us in. That's the only time I remember seeing my pa happy. But it didn't last long.

Momma didn't say nothing the whole time we was moving. She walked slow and had an unhappy look in her eyes. She was sad to be leaving Grandma, even though we wasn't moving very far. I think it scared her because she didn't have no place to run to in the country if she needed help.

The good thing for me and Dory was that Pa let us go outside more. He knew there wasn't no close neighbors to see the bruises we had pretty regular. The bad thing was Pa threw us around a lot more because there wasn't no one to see or hear. He done the same with Momma.

Me and Dory went exploring while the truck was unloaded. The old tool shed was the first thing we checked out. We pulled the door open, and it made a loud, screeching noise. Dory grabbed my hand and pressed tight up against me. There wasn't no light except what come through the door. It looked dirty like nobody had been in it for a long time. A rickety work bench set against one side: and there was a rusted saw, some big hammers, and an ax hanging on the wall above it. Dirty rags, empty paint cans, and spider webs was everywhere. A broke chair was leaning against the far wall, and thick dust covered everything.

Dory squeezed my hand hard and said, "I ain't going in there. There might be dead things."

"Me neither. Let's get out of here."

We run away as fast as we could without shutting the door. When we stopped running, we was standing in front of the root cellar. Dory looked up at me and said, "Should we peek in?"

I looked at Dory and all around us. The sun was out, and I didn't see nothing weird, so I said, "OK."

The door didn't stand straight up like a normal door. It laid down at an angle because it was built into a little hill: there was a pull handle in the middle on one side. I grabbed the handle and put all my weight into lifting it up. It didn't move. Dory grabbed hold and pulled too. It was heavy. With both of us putting all we had into it, we raised it up about half an inch. We give up and walked back to the house.

The inside of the house was dark. There wasn't many windows, and the few there was had some type of see-through curtains over 'em. Everything in the place was either black, brown, gray, or some other dark color. There wasn't nothing bright or cheerful anywheres.

Grandpa and Grandma was planning to rent a house in Florida that had furniture in it, so they left all their stuff for us to use. There wasn't much, and what was there looked like it had been wore pretty hard. Me and Dory got excited when we seen we each got our own bedroom. We never had that before. The trailer had a small room for us, and we slept in the same bed. Although we got kind of scared when we thought about being in a room in that house—alone. We felt safe when we was together.

Me and Dory started to scream when we seen a TV in the living room. But we stopped ourselves and didn't make a sound. We looked at each other, and a little smile crossed our mouths. We seen TV a few times when we was at Grandma's, and Pa was gone. Momma told us to never let Pa know we seen it. He didn't allow TV and would have beat us for sure if he knew. He'd of beat Momma too.

Pa was carrying a box through the front door and musta seen the look on our faces. He set the box down on the couch, walked over to the TV, pulled the plug from the wall, picked it up, and walked out the back door. Me and Dory looked down at the floor, walked to the porch, and set in old, plastic chairs that was left. We didn't move until Momma called us for lunch.

We seen Pa in the living room looking at a magazine with naked ladies in it. There was a bunch of empty beer cans setting on the table in front of him, and he had one clutched in his hand. As we walked by, he growled, "Don't you ever let me catch you watching TV."

Later that afternoon, I looked out the kitchen window and seen Pa setting on the ground with his back against the shed. Beer cans was scattered everywhere, and the box where he kept his crank was on the grass next to him. His cheeks was sunk in, his eyes looked like somebody painted black circles around 'em, and he didn't move. It looked like he was dead. I told Momma, and she said, "Just let him be. He'll be OK. We don't want to make him mad."

I guess Pa stayed the night outside because I didn't hear him come in. It's just as well he didn't. At least nobody got beat.

And that's how we spent the first day in our new house.

Chapter Ten

~~~~~~~~~~~~~~~~~~~~~~~~~~~~~~~~~~~~~

Pa liked being alone in the country. I guess it made him feel protected while he carried on with the crazy stuff he done. The rest of us wasn't happy about it. We missed being able to get away to Grandma's house them times when Pa would just set on the couch and shake or walk back and forth from one end of the house to the other or talk to people that wasn't there. Instead of going to Grandma's when Pa went nuts, we'd hide ourselves in another room, or set out on the porch when the weather was good. We set out a couple of times when it was snowing. We'd be freezing our butts off, but it was better than being around Pa.

Pa's truck was the only thing we had to get around, other than walking. But Momma wasn't allowed to drive it. We was stuck hoofing it when Pa took off and didn't come back for a few days. It didn't make no difference if he *was* home since he never took us anywhere.

Momma had to walk the two miles to town to keep her waitress job at Steiner's because Pa wouldn't drive her. She asked him to a few times, but she stopped askin' after he smacked her in the mouth and made her bleed. She walked in all kinds of weather: rain, snow, and scorching heat. She had to, or we wouldn't have had nothing to eat or money to keep the lights on. Pa spent what money he got from welfare and sellin' weed on booze and crack. Momma got lucky a few times and was picked up by a farmer who was heading into town. Whenever she got a ride home, she'd get dropped off down the road so Pa didn't see her. One-time, he seen her get out of a truck in front of the house and beat her for getting a ride. She never done *that* again.

Momma would take us to town with her and drop us at Grandma's if Pa was home and acting crazy. Me and Dory would be wore out by the time we made it to town. But we didn't mind none. We was so happy to be with Grandma. We could play, make noise, and do whatever we wanted.

A few times we seen cartoons on TV. My favorite was Popeye. It made me laugh when his arms got big after eating spinach. I wanted to be strong like him, so I could keep Pa from hurting Momma and Dory. I asked Momma to get me some spinach when she went to the market, but she never did. She knew Pa hated it and would just throw it away.

Grandma give me spinach one-time after I begged her for it. I didn't like it at all, but I made myself eat it. I run around trying to lift heavy stuff, but of course, nothing changed. I was a little kid and no match for my pa.

Momma hated to do it, but sometimes when Pa was more normal, she'd leave me and Dory at home with him while she worked. They was scary times. We never knew what he might do. Lots of times we'd set in the bedroom 'til Momma got back. We'd take turns tellin' stories to ourselves because we was too afraid to go outside and play. They was happy stories about princesses, puppies, and such. It helped us to get away in our minds.

Grandma Thelma would drive out to see us when she could, but that didn't happen much. Grandpa Earl drove heavy equipment for a town about twenty-five miles away and took the only car they had to get to work. He'd be tired and hungry when he got home, so Grandma tended to his needs.

The times she did come out, she'd turn around and go back if she seen Pa's truck was there. More than once I seen her stop in the trees before the yard opened up, set there for a minute, then back out of the drive. I wanted to run to her and tell her to come in. But I was too scared of what Pa would do if I did.

Winters was always the hardest. When Pa was home, he'd turn the heat way down. Sometimes he shut it off. He complained a lot about being too hot, even when it was freezing outside—and close to that in the house. He'd be sweating while the rest of us was shivering. Momma, me, and Dory would throw on all the warm clothes we could find to keep from freezing to death. I learned later it was the crank that made Pa so hot.

Over time, Pa's skin got grayer, and it sunk in all over his body, especially on his face. He had black rings around his eyes, and his teeth turned yellow-brown. A year after we moved to the country, he come home from wherever he'd went with a front tooth missing. It made him look scary and evil.

The sores on Pa's face and arms never went away. Blood would drip out after Pa scratched 'em. He did that a lot. His fingers would work them spots while he set on the floor staring into some other world mumbling gibberish to folks that wasn't there. Me and Dory would peek around the corner at him and hide ourselves in the bedroom, or run outside.

One day, after Momma had went to work and left me and Dory alone with Pa, we was running around the yard playing cops and robbers and seen the root cellar door was open. We run over to look inside, and a cool breeze was coming out of it. It was a hot day, and we was extra hot from running around. We crawled down the steps to cool off and see what was in there.

It wasn't big. I'd say eight-foot-long by four-foot-wide and high enough for a short person to stand. The floor, walls, and ceiling was dirt; and there was wood shelves on the walls. A few glass jars and some rusted tools set on the shelves: there was a handsaw without a handle, a pair of broke pliers, some bent nails, and an ice pick. It smelled of wet earth. There wasn't no light except what come in through the door.

Once we cooled down and seen what we wanted to see, me and Dory started up the stairs. Dory went first. She reached over to keep her balance and hit the stick holding up the door. It come crashing down and whacked Dory on the head. She fell back into me, and we both tumbled to the floor. Dory landed on top of me and didn't move. She got knocked unconscious for a few seconds, and I was kind of in shock.

It was pitch-black except for a little light shining through the cracks in the door. When she come to, blood was dripping from her head, and she started to cry. I run up the steps as fast as I could and started pushing on the door: it barely moved. I yelled for help 'til my voice give out. Nobody come for us. Pa was too strung out to hear us or too far gone to do anything about it if he did.

Momma come home late that day and freaked out when she seen Pa setting and staring into space, and us nowheres around. She run out the back door yelling our names, and as soon as we heard her, me and Dory started screaming for help. When the door come open, we run into Mamma's arms and hung on, crying. The warm air felt good after being in the cool cellar so long.

Momma took us in and cleaned us up. Dory's head wasn't cut too bad, so she didn't have to get stitches. I felt bad for her. Cleaning the cut with rubbing alcohol musta hurt worse than getting hit in the first place. Pa never asked where we was or what happened to us: he kept staring with that dead look to his eyes.

There was nights I could hear Pa shuffle down the hall and stop at Dory's room. The door'd creak open, then close. I never heard no sound come from the room until the door squeaked open a few minutes later, and Pa shuffled back to wherever he come from. I wanted to go to Dory, but I was too scared and would just lie there, froze. I didn't know if Momma was sleeping them times or was awake and too afraid to do anything. Nobody ever talked about what went on in Dory's room, but she'd be quiet the next day after them visits.

That's pretty much how life was in the country the first year or so. But it got worse—lots worse.

Chapter Eleven

~~~~~~~~~~~~~~~~~~~~~~~~~~~~~~~~~~~~~~~

I remember running into some boys from town one day in May: the year I was seven. I know it was May because Momma was trying to teach me and Dory some stuff about months. She said a lion comes in at the start of March, and a lamb runs out at the end. That didn't make no sense to me, and she laughed when I said I never seen a lion or lamb in the yard. A couple weeks later, I seen a lamb in a field down the road, so I figured Momma knew what she was talking about. She told us that rain showers in April brung flowers in May. To prove it, Momma pointed out the window to all the flowers growing around the yard and said, "Look! See all the pretty flowers grow-ing wild out there? That's because of all the rain we've been having."

After the month lesson, Momma and Do-ry started working in the kitchen, and I run outside to go exploring. Pa hadn't been around for a few days, and I felt kinda free. The sun was shining, a little breeze was blowing the grass around, and everything was green. It didn't get no better than that.

Grandma give me a shiny, red yo-yo the last time we was at her house, and I was working it as I walked down the drive that run to the road. I wasn't good yet, but I was starting to get the hang of it. A few times it come back up the string and landed in my hand like Grandma showed me. That was exciting. It was the only toy I had back then, and I kept it hid under my mattress so my pa wouldn't snatch it and throw it away.

Before I knew it, I was at the gravel road that run by the house. There was nothing on the road as far as my eyes could see in either direction. I seen the little flag was up on the mail box in front of our place. Momma told me that meant there was something in the box for us. I checked the flag every time I was near enough to see it. But I never seen it up before because nobody ever sent us nothing.

Shivers run through my body as I walked over to the box. I stood in front of it for a long time and stared up at the flag. I felt kind of scared too for what might be in there. After looking all around to make sure nobody was watching me, I grabbed the hook to open the door. I held it a bit, wondering if something was gonna jump out at me.

I gathered up all my courage, pulled hard on the hook, and the door flung open. At first I didn't see nothing. I went up on my tiptoes to get a better look, and there it was: the Hellridge paper. I knew right away what it was because I seen it over at Grandma's.

My hand shot in the box and grabbed the treasure. I pulled it out and checked around again to make sure nobody seen me. Somebody might have put it in there as a trick or something. I didn't know.

When I was sure I was alone, a smile come across my mouth. Finding that paper was as sweet as them times when Momma sneaked me a piece of hard candy from the tin she kept hid in the back of the kitchen cupboard.

I laid on my stomach in the tall grass next to the road with the paper laid out in front of me. I couldn't read too good, but I liked looking at the pictures.

There was a page with toys for sale at one of the local stores. I stared at that page for a long time and wondered what it would be like to play with them things. The BB gun picture held my eye the most. Ooh, to take it hunting in the woods by the house. Momma would be proud if I brung home a squirrel or rabbit for dinner.

My dreaming ended when I turned the page and seen a picture of my pa staring back at me. He looked dead with his hair stuck up every which way and them spots all over his face. His eyes was black holes, and there was something hung around his neck with the name of our town and a bunch of numbers wrote on it. I found out later that picture was took when they put him in jail.

I knew enough words to know he'd been caught by the cops for breaking into a car and taking some money. That's why he hadn't been home. He was sitting in jail waiting to see the judge. I remember wishing he'd get put in jail a long time, so we could live peaceful.

I was looking at his picture when I heard, "What ya doing." It give me the willies because I didn't hear no one come up on me. I rolled over quick and put my hand up to block the sun. There was three boys I never seen before looking down at me. I was too shook to say anything, so I kept staring at 'em.

The biggest boy give my foot a kick and said, "Hey! Are you deaf? I asked you a question."

I got up on my elbows to block the paper and said, "Nothing."

The shortest boy said, "That ain't possible. You gotta be doing something, unless you're dead. Is that it butt wipe? Are you dead?"

I didn't say nothing and squinted at him through the sun.

The big boy said, "He was doing something alright. He was looking at that paper behind him."

When I tried to grab the paper, the big boy dropped down on his knees and jerked it out of my hands. He glanced at it, seen the picture of my pa, and said, "So, you was reading about that druggie bum who busted into my dad's car! Well, I guess they got his sorry ass. Serves him right. He ain't nothing but trouble in this town."

Although I agreed, something inside me was boiling. I suppose it was because he was taking about *my* pa. I could say them things about him. But it wasn't right for others to do it.

Before I got myself in trouble saying something stupid, the third kid said, "Wait a minute! I know this guy. He used to live in a trailer across the street from my place. It's his dad that busted into your dad's car."

I froze as the big kid whipped his head around and glared at me. "Is that right, shithead? Was it your old man who stole from my dad?" I kept looking at him, trying not to cry, and too afraid to say anything. He grabbed me by my shirt, shook me hard, and yelled, "Is that right?"

The kid who thought he knew me, said, "That's him. I'm positive. He always looked like such a dork. I wouldn't forget."

The boy holding me cocked his arm and slugged me in the eye. I fell back on the grass. Stars was whirling around in my head, and I think I blacked out for a bit. The next thing I knew, the boys was standing over me, laughing. As they turned to go, the big one threw the paper in my face, pointed his finger at me, and said, "That's for what your old man done." Then he flipped me the bird, and they was gone.

I laid there trying not to cry, while tears of shame and hate flowed down my cheeks. I wanted to disappear and never see my pa or Hellridge again.

When I knew them boys was outta sight, I dragged myself up, got the paper, and walked back to the house. I put the paper on Momma's bed so she'd know where Pa was, then crawled into my bed and pulled the blanket over my head.

At lunch, Momma seen there was a red bump by my eye. I told her I run into a tree playing in the woods. She never said nothing about the paper, and I never said nothing about getting beat up.

Pa come back after serving thirty days in jail—nastier than ever.

Chapter Twelve

~~~~~~~~~~~~~~~~~~~~~~~~~~~~~~~~~~~~~

Our lives was changed forever a couple months after them boys beat me. Pa got out of jail after serving his thirty days and come back home angrier than a rattlesnake poked with a stick. He slapped Momma around more than usual. One-time he locked me and Dory in the shed for a whole day with no food or water. We both peed ourselves because we was scared of what Pa would do if he knew we messed in the shed. It was dark when he let us out. Lucky for us, our pants dried before he seen us, or he'd of beat us for sure.

Pa disappeared again after a couple weeks. We was all glad for the chance to be ourselves and not worry about what we said or done. As peace settled over us, our lives come crashing down.

August tenth was Momma's birthday. Grandma Thelma said the last time we visited her that she and Grandpa was coming out to see us and give Momma a present. They was planning to get there about eleven that morning.

Momma woke up early and was so excited she was humming songs. We all was excited. With Pa gone, we'd have Grandpa and Grandma to ourselves to do whatever we wanted.

Everybody took a shower and put on their best clothes. Momma wore a dress with flowers on it that she only put on for special times. She looked so beautiful. Dory was wearing a dress too. She was dancing all over the place and pretending to be a princess. That's the only time I ever remember seeing Dory in a dress. I wore a shirt with a collar. It was too big, but I liked it because it made me look older. My pants had a hole in the knee, but they was the nicest ones I had.

We went out on the porch to wait for Grandpa and Grandma when it got near eleven. It was a hot day, and we was too excited to set around in the house. Momma set on the steps with Dory on one side of her and me on the other. She told us stories about growing up in Hellridge, and the stuff she and her best friend, Pauline, done to cause mischief. Some of the stories was pretty funny. Me and Dory laughed and squeezed in closer to Momma. Pauline moved to California after high school, and Momma never heard from her. It's strange how people can be good friends, then go different ways and never be together again—like it never happened in the first place, except for the memories.

We heard the far-off sound of a siren over toward town. It was soft at first. Kinda sounded like a cat howling. Then it got louder and louder until it stopped out on the highway about a mile from the house.

Momma stopped in the middle of her story and went stiff. Me and Dory looked up at her. She was staring toward where the siren stopped and had a serious look on her face. I looked but didn't see nothing unusual. A second siren started up, then another. Momma whispered, "Oh no! Please, God! No!" She put her hands over her nose and mouth like she was praying.

I felt scared by the way Momma was acting. All of a sudden, she jumped up and started running down the drive. She stopped long enough to turn around and shout, "You kids go in the house and stay there until I get back!"

I was too worried about Momma to go back in the house and wait, so I got up and run after her. Dory come right behind me, and we run a whole mile without stopping. Momma was a little ways ahead because she was faster. I'll never forget her scream when she seen the car. It was the sound of a hundred hearts being tore apart.

A cop run up and grabbed her to keep her from running any farther. Me and Dory stopped right where we was, and I heard Momma yell, "Let me go. That's my mom and dad."

Grandpa and Grandma's car was upside down in the ditch with its front end all smashed in. A semitruck was stopped on the other side of the road. There was a big dent in its bumper. I looked back at the car and seen Grandpa hanging upside down by his seatbelt. He wasn't moving. There was a body lying in the road wearing a blue dress I seen Grandma wear before. I froze in place and thought I was gonna be sick. Dory was standing next to me and reached up for my hand.

I don't know how long we stood there. Everything kinda stopped and got fuzzy around me. My eyes narrowed down on that blue dress and refused to move: they was locked in place.

The next thing I remember is running as fast as I could back to the farm. I could hear Dory behind me crying, and hollering, "Wait up. Jakie, wait up."

A cop car pulled up and stopped as we was turning down the driveway. A lady cop got out and run to us. She dropped to her knees and pulled us close. She held us tight and kept making a shushing sound so we'd stop bawling. In between shushes, she whispered over and over, "You're safe. It's going to be OK." But deep inside I knew it wasn't gonna be OK. Life had changed in a flash, and it would never be OK again.

The lady cop put us in her car and drove to the house. She said she'd stay with us until Momma come back. We went inside and listened to her tell stories about when she was a little girl: the time her pony run away, and when she seen a tiny fairy flying around her back yard. Dory's eyes got big hearing about the fairy. She even give us some chocolate chip cookies she'd packed for her lunch. Me and Dory liked her a lot, and before long, we stopped shaking and sobbing.

Momma come back a few hours later riding in the back of another cop car. We run out on the porch and watched the car park in front of the house. Momma was staring out the window like she was someplace way far off. Her hair was kind of messed up, and her face was sunk in and sad looking. I never seen Momma look like that: even after she took a beating from Pa.

We run to Momma when she got out and threw ourselves around her. She hugged us tight, and we all cried.

The cops asked Momma if there was anything she needed. She looked up, and with a slight shake of her head, said, "No. Thank you. We'll be fine." Then another tear slid down her face.

The cops left, and we was alone—really alone.

Chapter Thirteen

~~~~~~~~~~~~~~~~~~~~~~~~~~~~~~~~~~~~~

It was quiet around our place after Grandpa and Grandma died. Nobody talked much. Momma wandered around like a zombie: when she wasn't setting on the porch, staring at the fields.

We ate good for a few days after the funeral because some of Grandma's neighbors brung us food. I never seen so much potato salad, biscuits, coleslaw, fried chicken, and pies. Me and Dory liked the pies best. I think Momma did too because that's something Pa never let us have. He said it was a waste of good money. I guess he liked the taste of weed and crank better.

One day, the guy who run the funeral parlor come to take Momma to town so she could get Grandpa and Grandma's burial clothes. When she come back, she brung some of the books we used to read at Grandma's. She hid 'em in the shed and told us we could only read 'em when we was sure Pa wasn't around.

Momma wanted to get a hold of Uncle Randy but didn't know where he lived or how to find him. He and Grandpa didn't get along too good ever since he swiped some cash when he was out for Momma's wedding. To this day, I don't think he knows his brother's dead.

Grandpa and Grandma's funeral was held five days after our lives come crashing down. I was scared to go, but Momma said we had to pay our last respects. I remember walking into the chapel like it was today. There was organ music playing, but I didn't see no organ. Momma held our hands as we walked to our seats. A few of Grandpa and Grandma's friends was there, and one lady was dabbing her eyes with a hanky.

When we was half way down the aisle, I looked up and seen two caskets at the front. I could see part of two faces. It freaked me out, and I froze where I stood. I knew them faces belonged to people I loved. Dory was too short and couldn't see 'em from where she was standing. She looked over and give me a strange look.

Momma kept walking to the front and pulled me and Dory along with her. We stopped at Grandpa first, and I started to shake. I thought I was gonna pee myself. I never seen a dead person before, let alone a dead person that was family. Dory couldn't see Grandpa and looked kind of confused by the way I was acting. When Momma picked her up, Dory let out a little scream and buried her face in Momma's neck.

Momma put Dory down and did the strangest thing I ever seen. With tears running down her cheeks, she bent down and put a kiss on Grandpa's forehead. That really did me up. I couldn't imagine kissing a dead person.

Dory kept pulling Momma's hand, trying to get away. But Momma drug us over to where Grandma was laid out. I looked away, so I'd only remember what she was like alive. Seeing Grandpa dead was a mistake. I didn't want the same for Grandma. Momma bent over and give Grandma a kiss too as Dory busted loose and run to her seat.

After seeing the caskets, we set down in the first row. I wished we could move to the back, far away from the dead bodies. But the organ music stopped, and the funeral guy stepped up and started saying stuff about Grandpa and Grandma. Momma kept sniffling and dabbing her eyes with a hanky while me and Dory set there looking down with our mouths hung open.

There was a big vase full of different-colored roses on the floor between Grandpa and Grandma. It was a hot day, and a fan was blowing to help keep the place a little cooler. The moving air pushed the smell of them roses up my nose and kept it there during the whole service. I've never cared much for roses since. They make me think of death.

The last thing the funeral fella read was something about the Lord being a Shepard who'd make me lie down in a pasture, then walk through a valley of death. I had no idea what he was talking about, but it sure scared the hell out of me.

After the service, we walked out of the chapel with the other folks. Two black station wagon-looking cars was parked out on the street in front of the place. I forget what they're called. We stood on the sidewalk for a bit, then a bunch of guys I didn't know walked out carrying one of the caskets. They loaded it into the first car, then went back in and brung out the other one. It was put in the second car.

Me, Momma, and Dory got in a car behind the casket cars with some lady I think was one of Grandma's friends. Momma talked to her like she knew her. The rest of the folks lined up behind us. The cars with Grandpa and Grandma started moving, and everybody followed 'em out of town to the graveyard.

Two holes was dug near a big tree at the top of a hill. The same guys who put Grandpa and Grandma in the cars, brung 'em out and set a casket over each hole. The funeral guy read some more stuff from a book while everybody stood around the holes. Some folks had tears running down their face.

While walking back to the car, I asked Momma what them big stones was scattered all over the ground. When she told me

they showed where dead people was buried,
I run the rest of the way to the car. As I got
in, I looked back up the hill to where
Grandpa and Grandma was. Two fellas I
didn't see before was lowering one of the
caskets into the hole. I wondered what was
gonna happen to my grandpa and grandma. Maybe this is what the funeral guy
meant when he talked about lying down in
a pasture.

The lady who give us a ride to the graveyard drove us back out to the farm. Nobody
said nothing the whole way. We was all
looking out the window, watching the world
blur by. As we pulled into the drive, fear
shot through my body. Pa's pickup was
parked next to the house. The car come to
a stop, and Momma sucked in a little
breath.

Chapter Fourteen

~~~~~~

We all walked into the house after the funeral kind of tense-like, not knowing what we was gonna find. Momma went first, then Dory, then me. As usual, Pa was setting on the couch with a beer in his hand, staring into whatever world he went to when he was drunk, drugged out, or both. He turned his head to Momma, and with a dead look in his eyes, said, "Heard Earl and Thelma's dead." That was it. He never said he was sorry or tried to give us comfort. At least he never hit us, screamed, or threw stuff. We was lucky for that. Momma stood there for a little, glaring at him with a look of hate on her face I never seen before, then walked to the bedroom with me and Dory right behind. I thought for sure he was gonna go after Momma for giving him that look. But he didn't.

A couple days after Grandpa and Grandma was buried, a fancy-looking car pulled down the drive, and a fella got out wearing a suit. That's something I hadn't seen much of before: a fancy car and a guy in a suit. He was a lawyer who come to talk to Momma.

He wanted to talk in private, but Pa refused to leave the room, or maybe he was too far gone to know what was going on. I don't know. Anyways, Momma took the lawyer out to the porch so they could talk. Turns out, Grandpa and Grandma give Momma their house. It was the only good thing that come out of the tragedy: if you can say anything from it was good.

After the lawyer drove off, Momma come back in the house, and I seen a sparkle in her eye that wasn't there before. Pa musta seen it too, because he said, "What that suit want?"

The spark dropped from Momma's eyes, and she didn't say nothing. She looked down at the floor, wringing her hands. That pissed Pa off, so he said, "I asked you something, woman. Now I'll ask it one more time. What did the suit want?"

Momma's voice was shaky, and she was breathing hard, when she said, "My mom and dad gave me the house."

Pa give out a chuckle, and with a smirk on his face, said, "Is that right? And what ya gonna do about it?"

Momma said, "I don't know. I just found out. But maybe we can move in and have a place of our own."

Pa raised his voice and said, "The hell you say. We got a place of our own. A good place. We ain't going nowhere. So get that dumb idea outta your head."

Momma didn't say nothing. She went to

the bedroom, and me and Dory followed her. When the door shut, Momma set down on the bed, put her hands over her face, and cried. Dory started to sob when she seen how sad Momma was, and I could feel tears building up too. Momma pulled us to her and hugged us tight. She said, "*Shhh*. Don't cry. It's going to be OK." That was the second time in a few days I heard them words: it's gonna be OK. Even though it come from Momma this time, I didn't believe it.

The morning after the lawyer come, Pa got in his pickup and drove off. He didn't say where he was goin' or when he'd be back, and we didn't ask. Momma was supposed to start back at Steiner's that day for the lunch shift, so she wrapped some of our favorite books in her apron, and we took off walking to town. We was sweaty by the time we got there, and the cool air inside felt good.

Momma set us in a booth at the back of the place while she went to talk to Mr. Steiner. Me and Dory knew Mr. Steiner from the other times we come in with Momma. Them other times, we was inside for a second while Momma got her coat or something, so we never set down.

Mr. Steiner was a nice guy. He wore big, thick glasses and was bald on top. He musta liked the food he cooked because he had the biggest belly I ever seen on a man. Me and Dory secret-smiled at each other every time we seen him. Momma liked working for him a lot, and he liked her too. He musta felt sorry for Momma with Grandpa and Grandma dead because he let us set in the booth the whole time she was working. It was fun watching her hurry around with big plates of food and talking to people I never seen before.

We finished our books and was looking around at all the people when Mr. Steiner come and give us each a coloring book and box of crayons. We couldn't believe he done that and just set there staring at him with our mouths hung open. Momma walked by and said, "What do you say?"

Together we said, "Thank you, Mr. Steiner."

Coloring was the funnest thing we done in a long time. I don't know how long we colored, but the next time I looked up Mr. Steiner was at the table again. He had two big, juicy hamburgers, two plates of fries, and two cups of ice-cold coke. We put ketchup and mustard all over the burgers and squirted a big mess of ketchup on the fries. Me and Dory agreed it was the best lunch we ever had. By the time we was done, we had ketchup and mustard smeared from cheek to cheek and all over our hands. It took a pile of napkins to get it off.

After her shift was done, Momma tried to

pay Mr. Steiner for our food, but he wouldn't take her money. He said, "It's my pleasure. They're such good kids." I don't remember anybody ever calling us good kids except Momma and Grandma. But they was family and Mr. Steiner wasn't. That made it kind of special.

After thanking Mr. Steiner and shaking the big, beefy hand he stuck out at us, we walked out the door after Momma.

When we got on the sidewalk, Momma stopped and looked down the street toward home. She tuned, started walking the other way, and said, "Come on. Let's go to Grandma's house and see if we can find some things to take home.

Me and Dory walked fast to keep up, and we give each other a strange look. We was kinda scared of going in the house after they was dead, and we didn't know what Pa might do if he found out. But Momma kept on walking, and we kept on following. Neither of us made a peep about our fear.

It didn't take long to get there, and we didn't slow down 'til we got to the porch. Momma put the key in the door, took a deep breath, and in we went. It was strange being there without hearing Grandma say something like, "Well, look who's here." She said stuff like that every time we come to visit.

The place was hot, and the air was dead. Other than that, it seemed like Grandma could have walked in any time. Nothing had been touched since the day Grandpa and Grandma left to come to our place. The town paper was on the arm of Grandpa's chair like he always left it, and his slippers was setting on the floor in front of the chair. Two kitchen chairs was pulled out from the table. There was a plate with a half-eaten piece of moldy toast on the table in front of one chair, and a half glass of cottage cheese-like milk on the table in front of the other. A few dishes was in the sink, and Grandma's apron was hanging on a hook by the fridge.

Me and Dory set quite on the kitchen chairs while Momma was walking around looking for stuff we might use. Other than Momma's footsteps, the only other sound was Dory's foot hitting the chair as she swung her leg back and forth. That musta been her way of showing her fear. Mine was pumping my leg up and down. I felt like I was glued in place and kept looking back-and-forth between the moldy toast and rotten milk. I couldn't help wondering who'd been eating the toast and who'd been drinking the milk.

Momma finished collecting stuff and set it on the table. There was a couple of bras, two dresses, a pair of blue jeans, and Grandma's red tennis shoes. There was no clothes in the pile for me and Dory because we was too small for any of it to fit. A tiny glass bird was in the pile too. Momma give it to Grandma when she was a little girl, and Grandma kept it ever since. When Momma looked up at us, a big smile crossed her mouth. She stuck her hand in her waitress apron and pulled out a deck of playing cards. We was so excited. We jumped out of our chairs and run to grab the cards. Before giving 'em to us, Momma jerked her hand back, and said, "We'll have to hide the cards with the books and play with them when your dad isn't there. OK?" Of course, we agreed.

Some paper grocery bags was stuck in between the wall and the fridge. Momma pulled out two bags and stuffed the clothes, bird, and cards in one and handed it me to carry home. She filled the other bag with a bunch of canned goods: spam, green beans, spinach, peas, red beats, peaches, and pears. Then she give Dory a pack of napkins so she'd have something to carry too.

As we stepped out on the porch, I felt like the luckiest boy on the earth. It was like we won a big prize or something. The walk home went quick. All I could think about was playing with them cards—and maybe trying spinach again. I thought if I give it a second shot, I might get strong like Popeye.

Chapter Fifteen

~~~~~~~~~~~~~~~~~~~~~~~~~~~~~~~~~~~~~~

The time Dory turned six was a special time and a bad time all rolled together. I was eight and feeling like the man of the house because Pa was either not there or too messed up to make a difference. We all got swore at and pushed around them times Pa was out of his mind, which was usual. And Momma always seemed to have a bruise on some part of her body or other.

Me and Dory woke up extra early on her birthday. I'd have slept longer, but my sister come in and kept whispering my name and poking me on the nose. She was excited to see what present she'd get. I don't blame her. I was excited on my day too.

We set on my bed talking until we heard Momma walk down the hall to the kitchen. Then Dory run out with me right after. Momma was at the stove in her brown terry robe, and Dory, busting with excitement, grabbed her around the legs from behind. Momma turned, picked up my sister in her arms, and said, "Well, Missy, what are you so happy about? Huh? Could it be your birthday?"

Dory pressed Momma's cheeks together between her hands and made her mouth look like a fish. And with her nose inches from Momma's nose, stared deep into her eyes, and whispered, "Yes it is. It is my birthday. Did you forget?"

Momma's face took on a smile, and she said, "Why yes, I must have."

Pulling Momma's face closer, Dory said, "No you didn't. I know you didn't. You'd never forget my birthday."

Momma set her back on her feet and said, "Well, maybe I didn't. You'll have to see. Why don't you set the table while I whip up some special pancakes?"

Dory put out four plates and glasses for juice while I laid down paper napkins, a knife, and a fork at each place. Pa was sleeping, but we set a spot for him too in case he come out. If he seen nothing was put out for him, he'd get mean and nasty: stuff could get broke or somebody slapped around for forgetting him. We didn't want nothing to ruin Dory's big day.

The smell of bacon frying made the place feel happy and got my mouth watering. Momma told us to set as she put a huge pancake and two pieces of bacon on each plate. She made the cakes to look like Minnie Mouse with big ears and a bow on her head. The eyes, nose, and big smiley face was made out of banana slices. Dory's eyes lit up when she seen Minnie, and she jumped up to give Momma a hug. When the orange juice was poured and the syrup bottle set on the table, we all dug in. Dory waited a minute because she didn't wanna ruin Minnie. But hunger got the best of her, and she cut off Minnie's bow—grinning from ear-to-ear.

Momma cleaned off the table when the last of the breakfast disappeared. She told Dory to stay in her chair and not turn around. Dory give me a quick look and scrunched up her face with excitement. She knew something good was coming.

I seen Momma reach in the cupboard above the fridge and pull down a chocolate cake that Mr. Steiner give her when she was at work. There was six candles stuck in the top, and the words HAPPY BIRTHDAY, DORY was spelled out with pink frosting. Momma told Dory to close her eyes and not peek. She lit the candles and put it on the table in front of the birthday girl. Then me and Momma sung Happy Birthday. Dory opened her eyes, let out a squeal, and clapped her hands. She blew out all the candles with one breath while she laughed and bounced in her chair. It was one of them rare times when Pa was out of our minds for a minute, and we was really happy.

Momma give Dory a table knife to cut the cake, and she put down clean plates to serve it on. Dory set a big slice on each plate before licking the frosting off the knife. We couldn't believe it when Momma pulled a box of vanilla ice cream out of the freezer. I couldn't remember the last time we had ice cream. It musta been over at Grandma's.

Momma got up as we finished our cake and went over to the pan drawer next to the stove. She pulled out a big box wrapped in pink paper with pictures of kittens and puppies on it, and a white bow was stuck on the top. She handed it to Dory and said, "Happy birthday, honey!"

Dory let out another squeal as she reached for the present and said, "It's so big. What is it Mommy?"

"Well, I think you should open it and find out."

The paper and ribbon come off in a heartbeat. Dory sucked in a little breath when she pulled off the top of the box and seen the fancy pink dress with frilly stuff around the neck and sleeves. She took it out and said, "Oh Momma, it's so pretty," before she started to bawl like the little girl she was.

Dory jumped up to go put on her new dress when we heard Pa come out of the bedroom and shuffle down the hall. Dory set back down and put the top on the dress box. We all froze with our eyes turned down at the table, scared of what might come next.

Pa come in the kitchen and stopped when he seen us. I peeked up at him and seen him staring at the cake with a dead look in his eyes. His hair was messed up and he hadn't shaved in days. He looked how I thought a real-life zombie would look.

Pa let out a grunt and said, "What's the cake for? It's breakfast time."

Momma got up to start pancakes for him and said, "It's a special day. It's Dory's sixth birthday."

"No shit? How about that?"

Then Pa set down hard in his chair, let out a big belch, scratched his hairy belly, and started eating Dory's cake. By the time his pancakes was ready, the cake was gone. He set there glaring at Dory while she kept looking down at the table. He never wished her a happy birthday or nothing. After chugging down a glass of orange juice, he got up from the table, threw on the same dirty T-shirt and jeans he'd been wearing for days, and left.

Dory was heart broke, and she started to sob. Momma hugged her tight and kept kissing her hair all over. "Don't cry, honey. Your daddy loves you. He's just going through a bad time right now and doesn't know how to show it. And you know how much Jakie and I love you? More than all the stars in the sky and flowers in the whole world."

The rest of the day was quiet. But the shine was outta Dory's eyes. I felt hate for my pa.

Chapter Sixteen

~~~~~~~~~~~~~~~~~~~~~~~~~~~~~~~~~~~~~

Spring come early the year I was nine. I guess Punxsutawney Phil didn't see his shadow; or maybe he did; I forget how that's supposed to go. By June it was pretty hot, and me and Dory was kind of bored. Momma was working a lot at Steiner's, so we'd have food, clothes, and keep the lights on. Pa didn't contribute nothing to us. Whatever he got from welfare and selling weed was used to buy more meth. He'd come and go at all times of the day or night. When he was home, me and Dory would either stay in our rooms or go outside to be as far away from him as possible. It was never a good idea to cross paths with him. Them times he was gone, we'd set out on the porch and make up stories about magical places, wander around the yard trying to catch butterflies, or play with them cards we got from Grandma's.

One day Momma come in from work carrying a letter she got out of our mailbox. I was surprised when I seen it because nobody ever sent us nothing in the mail. It turned out to be from Aunt Mary: Pa's younger sister from Valentine, Nebraska. She wasn't married, didn't have no kids, and was wondering if me and Dory would like to come stay with her for a while.

We was so excited thinking about going someplace different: we could barely stand it. Momma knew Aunt Mary from the time she lived in Hellridge. That was before she got knocked up by some boy passing through on vacation and was forced to leave home to save her family from shame. I heard the baby died before it was born. Leastways, that's the story that was passed around. She didn't come back home after that and started a life on her own in Nebraska. She was sixteen.

Momma said she liked Aunt Mary and felt sorry for her that she got kicked out of her family when she was just a kid. It was after Momma and Pa was hitched that Aunt Mary disappeared from town. Pa never talked about her, and I don't think he seen her since she left. Of course, he never talked about nothing, unless it was to put us down.

Me and Dory dug an old suitcase out of Momma's closet that she took from Grandpa and Grandma's house after they died. We started packing stuff we thought we'd need for the trip: T-shirts, jeans, underpants, tennis shoes, socks, tooth brushes, and a comb. When nobody was looking, I stuck them playing cards under the clothes.

Pa come home later that day and seemed

about as normal as he'd been in a long time. So Momma said, "Paul, your sister invited the kids to come stay with her for a while, and I was wondering if you could drive them down?"

"My sister? Mary? Hell, I didn't think she was still alive. Where's she living?"

"Valentine, Nebraska. It's a couple hundred miles south of here, just across the border."

"Whoa! I ain't putting that kind of miles on my truck. And I never want to see that bitch again after what she done." He walked out back by the shed. Ten minutes later the look of death had returned.

Momma called Aunt Mary from Steiner's the next day and made plans for the three of us to go see her on Friday. That was in two days. Momma was off on Saturday, and she traded her Friday with another waitress so she could take us and have some time to get us settled at Aunt Mary's.

Me and Dory didn't sleep much Thursday night. Momma had three tickets on a Greyhound bus that was to leave at eight-thirty Friday morning. I seen them buses a few times when we was walking into town, and I always wondered what it would be like to ride one. I figured you had to be rich to travel like that. And we was gonna ride one ourselves. It made me feel special.

Pa wasn't around when we got up on Friday, so we quick ate breakfast and hurried down the road so's not to miss the bus. I don't remember walking to town. My mind was fixed on our big adventure.

The bus hadn't come yet when we got to the station, so we set on a bench out front to wait. There was four or five other folks waiting too. My jaw dropped down when the bus pulled in. It was a lot bigger than I remembered. Of course, I never been close to one before. Only seen 'em at a distance out on the highway.

The door opened, and the driver walked down the steps and into the station. He looked like a pretty important guy to me. I figured he musta been to be able to drive that big bus. When he finished what he needed to do inside, he come back out and started putting the bags and boxes under the bus.

Momma showed our tickets to the driver as we was getting on. Dory went first, then me, then Momma. I remember looking around as I started up the steps to see who was watching us. I hoped them boys who beat me up was there. That would show 'em who the big guy was.

The air was cool inside the bus, and the seats was big. Dory set next to the window, and I set next to her. Momma set across the aisle from me. I couldn't believe how high up we was off the street. It was nothing like riding in a car or Pa's pickup.

The next thing I knew, the driver got on,

the doors slid shut, there was a hissing sound like the rush of air, and we was off.

Chapter Seventeen

~~~~~~~~~~~~~~~~~~~~~~~~~~~~~~~~~~~~~

The bus trip to Aunt Mary's was the first time I'd been more than two miles from Hellridge. I couldn't believe how big the world was. Seemed like we was riding forever. We had to stop at six little towns along the way to pick up or drop off folks.

At the second stop the driver took a little break, so we had time to get off the bus and walk around a bit. There was a mom-and-pop market across the road, and Momma asked us if we'd like to go check it out. Of course we jumped at the chance to explore. Anything to do something new and different.

When we walked in, there was a little old man, bald as a bowling ball, helping a lady put her groceries in a paper sack. The place had a smell about it like nothing I'd ever smelled before. It was a mixture of candy, vegetables, meat, and dust. Me and Dory couldn't believe our luck when Momma walked over to the freezer and said, "Would you guys like to try a Fudgsicle?"

I didn't know what that was, but we both said, "Yes."

Momma bought three of 'em, one each. It was like nothing I ever had before: ice-cold, chocolaty stuff froze to a stick. I thought it was ice cream at first. But Momma said it wasn't. Whatever it was, it tasted good and was the perfect treat for a hot summer day. By the time we was finished, me and Dory had chocolate running down our chins and all over our hands. Before we got back on the bus, Momma took us in the restroom at the bus stop so we could clean up.

I set next to the window for the next part of the trip, and Dory set in the seat by the aisle, across from Momma. As we was about to pull out, the driver popped the door open, and this weird looking guy come on. He reminded me of my pa with his long, dirty hair and them dark circles around his eyes. He walked down the aisle, and when he was a few seats from us, I seen his eyes lock on Momma. I quick looked over at Momma, but she was busy looking at some paper she'd picked up in the store.

I was hoping the guy would keep moving to the back of the bus. But when he got next to Momma, he seen the empty seat next to her and slid into it. That made me nervous. I could smell him when he come by. It was the same B.O. and booze stink Pa always carried around with him.

I don't think I looked out the window the whole time that guy was on the bus. I'd look over at him every few seconds to make sure he wasn't bothering Momma. He kept looking out of the corner of his eye at

Momma's legs, then up to her chest. I wanted to get up and go punch him in the mouth. I remember thinking how much I wanted a can of spinach to help me puff up big and strong.

Momma kept reading whatever it was she got from the store and didn't pay no attention to him. A few times she looked down the aisle to the front of the bus or over at me and Dory. It wasn't long before she leaned away from the guy. I guess the smell was getting to her too.

As luck would have it, the weirdo got off at the next stop. After he was off, Momma made me and Dory crack up when she looked over, wrinkled up her face, and pinched her nose with her fingers. A pretty, young girl got on and took the seat next to Momma for the rest of the trip. I was free to relax and look out the window.

I seen stuff I never seen before. As we was passing through one small town, there was a house with a big yard, and in the middle of the yard was a huge tank filled to the top with water. There was wood steps so you could get in the water, and a slide you could slip down to make a splash. A boy and girl about me and Dory's age was jumping up and down in the pool and throwing a huge red-and-white-striped ball back and forth. Me and Dory looked at each other and agreed we wanted one of them in our yard someday.

The driver come on and announced the next stop was Valentine, Nebraska, and we'd be there in about thirty minutes. I looked out the window and seen an animal I never seen before standing by the fence that run alongside the road. It looked like a cow, but it had big, pointy horns that stuck out at least three foot on each side of its head. I quick looked at Momma and said, "Did you see that animal with them big horns?"

"I did."

"What was it? A cow?"

"Yes, it is a cow. It comes from the state of Texas and is called a Texas Longhorn. There aren't many of them around here. You're lucky to get to see one."

I kept staring out the window, and it wasn't long before we passed a big sign that said WELCOME TO NEBRASKA. I said, "Momma, we're in Nebraska. A whole new state."

"I know. I saw the sign too. It won't be long now and we'll be at Aunt Mary's."

Momma was right because it wasn't but a few minutes later I seen a sign that said VALENTINE. As we was driving through town, I couldn't help but notice there was red valentines everywhere: on the side of buildings, in store windows, and even painted on the sidewalk in some places.

The bus went most of the way through town before pulling into a Conoco gas station. I figured we was gonna get gas, but it turned out to be the bus station too. As we come to a stop, I seen a kinda plump lady jumping up and down next to the bus and waving her arms like a crazy person. I said, "Momma, look at that crazy lady jumping all over the place."

Momma stood up so she could see out the window, and a big grin spread across her face. She said, "That's your Aunt Mary," and started waving back at her.

It took a minute for us to get our stuff together and wait for the people in front of us to get off. Aunt Mary was standing right outside the door and put Momma in a bear hug the minute she stepped off the bus. She and Momma cried and laughed at the same time.

Once she finished with Momma, Aunt Mary dropped to her knees and pulled both me and Dory into the biggest pair of boobs I ever seen. I could barely breathe and was glad when she finally let us go.

That's how it started: one of the best and worse times I ever had.

Chapter Eighteen

~~~~~~

When all the hugging was done, and Momma and Aunt Mary wiped the last tears outta their eyes, I grabbed our suitcase with both hands and followed Aunt Mary to her truck. Her ride was a 1975 Ford pickup, faded-yellow except where the rust had ate through. It was missing the back bumper and had the biggest tires I ever seen on a pickup.

Momma helped me lift the suitcase into the truck bed and got in the cab with Aunt Mary. Me and Dory started to climb in next to Momma, when Aunt Mary said, "Why don't you two jump in the back with the suitcase?"

I give Momma a quick look to see if it was OK. She nodded and said, "Go on. I used to ride in the back of my dad's truck when I was a little girl. It's fun."

Me and Dory run around to the back, but we couldn't get in because there wasn't no bumper. Aunt Mary called out, "Use the tire." I pulled Dory up so she could step on the tire and drag herself in. Then I jumped in. We set with our backs to the cab and each flung an arm over the side to hang on. Aunt Mary's house was only a little ways from the bus station, but it was the funnest ride I ever had. Me and Dory couldn't stop smiling as we bounced down the road to the house.

Aunt Mary lived at the edge of town in a little white house she rented from the owner of the Niobrara Market where she worked as a cashier. I heard her tell Momma rent was cheap because she'd worked at the market since moving to Valentine, and her boss liked her. The house needed painting pretty bad, but me and Dory didn't care. We was happy to be outta Hellridge and on an adventure.

It was after lunch by the time we got to the house, and my stomach was gurgling from excitement and hunger. Aunt Mary told me to take the suitcase to the bedroom me and Dory was sharing and said, "How'd you like a grilled cheese sandwich for lunch?"

I didn't know what that was, but it sounded good, and I said, "Sure. I'm starving."

"Great! We'll have a feast. You and Dory go wash your hands after you drop the suitcase and come in the kitchen."

While Aunt Mary fixed lunch, she and Momma jawed about things they done when they was little girls, what it was like living in Valentine, and all kinds of stuff I hadn't heard before. I wanted to know what a grilled cheese sandwich was, so I stood by the stove and watched. I remember clear as day how Aunt Mary made it. She put a square pan-like thing on the stove, melted a bunch of butter all over it, and set four slices of Wonder Bread in the butter. Then she cut pieces of Velveeta cheese, laid 'em on the bread, put another slice of bread over the cheese, and pressed each one with a fork. I seen the cheese was starting to melt when Aunt Mary flipped the sandwiches to the other side. When they was done, she put 'em on a plate next to a big slice of dill pickle.

That was the first time I ate Velveeta cheese and dill pickles. I liked 'em both a lot and gobbled down three pickle slices. I could have ate another sandwich, but I was too shy to ask, not knowing Aunt Mary too good yet. But it didn't make no difference: she set a tin of fresh-baked chocolate chip cookies on the table. Aunt Mary said she pulled 'em out of the oven before she come to get us. They was big, and I ate four before Momma said I had enough.

After a bit, Momma said, "Jakie, why don't you clear off the table for Aunt Mary? Dory you can help too."

Me and Dory jumped up. I put the plates in the sink, and Dory threw the paper napkins in the trash. I moved the cookie tin to the counter by the fridge and sneaked two more cookies: one for me and one for Dory. When I turned around, Momma give me the evil eye, which was more funny than evil, and said, "I saw that, mister." As I reached up to put 'em back, Momma said, "OK. Just this once. Run along now you two and go play."

It was easy being at Aunt Mary's. There was a kind of peace about it. The cloud that always hung over us was gone, and I hoped it wouldn't never come back. Aunt Mary was smiley and happy all the time. I felt good being around her. Momma laughed and talked more than before, except maybe early on at Grandma's.

Aunt Mary was an artist of sorts, and the pictures she done was hanging all over the walls of her house. They was colorful and cheery with no real shape to 'em: like a dog or horse or person. She called 'em abstract something or other. I never seen nothing like 'em before, but I liked how they made me feel.

In the evening after the sun went down, Aunt Mary said, "What would you guys like to do?"

I grinned and said, "I brung a pack of playing cards. Do you wanna play Go Fish?"

Aunt Mary said, "Oh, I haven't played that in years," as she plopped down on the floor in front of the couch. "Tell me the rules again. I'm not sure I remember how it goes."

Go Fish was the only card game me and

Dory played when Momma worked and we was alone. We never got tired of it.

The four of us played six games. Dory won three; I won two; Momma won one. With that, Aunt Mary said, "OK already! You guys are too good for me. I can't take any more defeat. I'm going to bed so we can get up tomorrow and have a fun day exploring Valentine."

Me, Momma, and Dory was tired after getting up early and riding the bus for two hundred miles. We washed up, and everybody went to bed. Me and Dory never even talked after we got in bed. I don't remember falling asleep, but it was the best sleep I had in a long time.

The next morning after breakfast, we all got in the truck and drove Momma back to the Conoco bus station. She'd stayed long enough to get us settled and had to get back to work. Aunt Mary give her a big hug and said, "We've got to get together more often. Family is so important, and you guys are all I've got."

"We will. Promise. I love you, Mary." Momma dabbed her eyes with the back of her hand, give me and Dory a long squeeze, and kissed us. "I'll see you in a couple weeks. Be good for your aunt. Love you!"

Momma got on the bus and took a seat by the window where we was standing. We kept waving and blowing kisses to each other. As the bus was pulling out, Momma pointed to her eye, made a heart shape with her hands, and pointed to us.

Me, Dory, and Aunt Mary watched the bus until it disappeared around the corner.

Chapter Nineteen

~~~~~~~~~~~~~~~~~~~~~~~~~~~~~~~~~~~~~~

When Momma's bus disappeared around the corner, Aunt Mary said, "OK you two, let's go have some fun. You wanna go play in the park?"

Together we hollered, "Yes."

"I'll race you to the truck. If you beat me, I'll buy you an ice cream."

That's all it took for me and Dory to take off runnin' like the wind. I touched the truck first, then Dory. I don't know how hard Aunt Mary tried, but she come up way last. Of course, being on the plump side didn't do her no favors.

The city park was at the edge of town. I couldn't believe how big it was. Nothing like the little park in Hellridge. There was tall trees, trails you could walk on, and even a place where you could take a shower if you wanted.

We walked down to a little creek that run through the park. Me and Dory took off our shoes, rolled up our pant legs, and waded in. Aunt Mary did it too. The water was cool and felt good on my skin. I remember how the mud squished up between my toes.

Aunt Mary pointed to a spot where the water was clear as glass and said, "Look!

There's a big old fish next to the log."

Sure enough. There it was. The biggest fish I ever seen. To be honest, it was the only fish I ever seen, except for cooked ones served at Steiner's. We walked around looking for more fish, but never seen any.

As we was getting out of the water, Dory let out a scream that made me and Aunt Mary jump. She pointed to the far bank and said, "There's a frog setting right next to the water." Sure enough, it was setting there still as a picture. "Do they bite? Do they have poison in 'em?"

Aunt Mary give out a little laugh and said, "No, honey. It's not going to bite you, unless you're a little bug it wants to eat for lunch. And there aren't any poisonous frogs around here. You don't have to worry. That little guy won't hurt you." That seemed to make Dory feel better, but she kept lookin' back at the thing as we put on our shoes and walked to the truck.

There was a little lake cross the road from the park, and I asked Aunt Mary, "Can we go see the lake?"

"You bet. Let's do it."

The lake had a boat dock, and a boy about my age was standing at the end, fishing. I wished I could have a try at fishing. I heard about it, but never got the chance to do it. Pa wasn't into fishing, or much of anything else other than crank and booze. And we didn't have a fishing pole.

After the lake, Aunt Mary drove us a ways out on the other side of town to a wide-open prairie where wild animals was roaming free. It was cool. We drove through the place and seen a herd of buffalo, a herd of elk, and a prairie dog town. I'd heard before there was buffalo around, but I didn't really believe it. Man, them things are big. One walked right up to the car and stood lookin' in the window at me. It kind of freaked me out, but Aunt Mary said not to worry, we was safe as long as we stayed in the truck. I never even heard of elk before. We didn't get too close to 'em, but close enough I could tell the bulls' antlers was huge. I seen a prairie dog before out by the farm, but only one. This was a whole town of 'em. Heads was popping up and down all over the place. There musta been a million.

Driving back to town, Aunt Mary said, "Is there anything you can think of that we still need to do?"

Me and Dory thought for a bit but couldn't think of nothin'. I said, "Nothin' that I know of. We already done a lot."

"Well, OK then. I guess we can forget about the ice cream I promised."

"No way!" me and Dory shouted together.

"Oh, so you do think we need to do something else." Aunt Mary looked at her watch and said, "It's about lunch time. What do you say we take a spin over to the Frosty Drive In and get us some burgers, fries, and a shake?"

All me and Dory could say was, "Yeah! Yeah! Yeah! Yeah!"

I don't know if it was because I was starving or not, but they was the best burgers I ever had. Even better than the ones Mr. Steiner give us. The fries was good too. And the chocolate shakes was another first for me and Dory. We'd had ice cream a few times before, but nothing as good as them shakes.

After all we done that morning, and with our bellies full, we decided that going home for a nap sounded pretty good.

The next morning, I finished washing the breakfast dishes, and Aunt Mary said, "How'd you guys like to take a picnic lunch and walk down to the Niobrara River? It's only about a mile from here."

I said, "Sure!"

Dory said, "Can we make peanut butter 'n' jelly sandwiches to bring with us?"

"Absolutely. And I'll throw in some apples, sodas, and if you want, a few of the chocolate chip cookies."

"Yes! Cookies!" shouted Dory, as she reached in the cupboard to get down the peanut butter and jelly.

"And be sure to bring your swim suits"

"We don't got any," I said, and looked down with shame.

"Not to worry. You really don't need one anyway. Your undies ought to do just fine."

"Not our undies," cried Dory, as she turned to look at Aunt Mary with a look of horror on her face.

"It's no big deal. Undies look just like a swim suit. Besides, there probably won't be any other people where we're going."

Dory didn't say nothing, but the look on her face eased some.

We took the gravel road that run out back of the house. There was no cars on it, and we was at the river before I knew it. Dory pert near skipped the whole way. It was the prettiest spot I ever seen. The high bank on the other side of the river was green and covered with big trees, mostly pine. I remember the sky was bluer than I ever seen it before, and a few white clouds was floating above. The river wasn't deep and flowed slow.

There was a sand bar in the middle of the river, and since there wasn't other people around, me and Dory stripped down to our skivvies and wadded out. Aunt Mary took off her shoes, rolled up her pant legs, and come out with us. It felt good with the cool water running against my legs and the warm sun beatin' down on my back. It was perfect.

Aunt Mary had to go back to her job at the market on Monday, but she told us we could walk around town or to the river if we got bored staying at home. Only thing was, we had to stay together. Every morning before she took off, she left a couple dollars on the kitchen table so we could get an ice cream or something while she was gone. Every day we was there, me and Dory went to the Frosty Drive In for ice cream or to the market to see Aunt Mary and buy candy.

The two weeks with Aunt Mary was the best time of my life. I think it was for Dory too. Except for how they ended.

Chapter Twenty

~~~~~~~~~~~~~~~~~~~~~~~~~~~~~~~~~~~~

My friend Dorothy come over to check on me this morning. She does that a lot since I moved in to Grandma and Grandpa's old house. We walked down to the Save & Go at the end of the block for an ice cream bar and to get some air. Like I said before, Dorothy knows about my PTSD and the trouble I have trusting people and being close to 'em. This time before she turned around to leave, she put her arms around me and give me a quick hug. It's the first time in years I didn't feel like crawling outta my skin when somebody touched me. I guess I'm starting to feel comfortable with her. Maybe talking into this machine is helping too.

Anyways, back to my time with Aunt Mary.

Me and Dory was planning to take the bus back to Hellridge after being at Aunt Mary's for two weeks. Aunt Mary was gonna tell the bus driver we was traveling alone and to keep an eye on us 'til we got home. Momma said she'd meet us at the station when the bus pulled in.

The day before we was to leave, I woke up with a start when I heard loud banging on the front door. Dory's eyes popped open, and we laid in our beds staring at each other. Dory looked scared, and I was feeling it too.

Aunt Mary come out of her bedroom and walked down the hall to the door. As soon as she opened the door, I heard her say, "Paul! What are you doing here?"

I didn't hear no reply, just a shocked, "Paul," from Aunt Mary. Then the door slammed shut.

I felt like I was gonna barf. My stomach got all knotted up, and shudders run up and down my body. Dory fell back on the bed and pulled the blanket up over her head. I could hear her sobbing. The best time I ever had quick turned to the worst.

I heard his footsteps coming down the hall. Aunt Mary was right near him and said, "Paul get out of here. You don't belong here."

Pa yelled, "Shut up!" Then the sound of flesh getting hit hard echoed through our room. I heard what sounded like a body hitting the floor, but no other words was spoke. I knew he'd hit Aunt Mary and knocked her down.

I was so scared I peed myself. There was a rock setting on the table next to my bed that I brung back from the river the last time we was there. I don't know why I done it, but I grabbed it, squeezed it hard, and cocked my arm back. It give me a little feeling of power, like I could protect us.

The footsteps stopped outside the bed-room door. My arm started shaking from fear and the weight of the rock in my hand.

A raspy, drunken voice said, "Hello, kids. Guess who? I come to get you and take you back home." The knob on the door started to turn. I cocked my arm back more. The door opened a crack, and Dory give out a little cry. When the door swung all the way open, I flung the rock at my pa. My aim wasn't so good, and the rock slammed into the door frame, leaving a great big dent and some missing paint.

Pa come barreling in the room and headed straight for me with a look that had kill wrote all over it. I tried to jump to the other side of the bed to get away from him, but his arms was too long. He caught my hand and jerked me down hard to the floor. The side of my head hit first, and I thought I was gonna pass out. There was a bloody spot on the floor where my head landed.

Dory kept still under her blanket. Pa stood there looking down at us. The stink he always carried was all over the room. I was too scared to move but glad he didn't tear into me no more.

After what seemed like an hour, Pa said, "You two throw on some clothes and get the hell outta here." He slammed the door, and I heard him mumble something to Aunt Mary.

I got up fast and grabbed my shirt and pants off the chair. Dory still hadn't moved or said nothing. I went to her bed, and whispered, "Come on, Dory. Get up. Get dressed. Let's get outta here before Pa comes back to beat us some more."

Dory stuck her head out from under the blanket and said, "Where we gonna go?"

I said, "Let's head down to the river. He ain't gonna find us there. Maybe he'll leave after a bit."

When we come outta the bedroom, Aunt Mary was setting on the couch with Pa standing over her. There was blood by the corner of her mouth. She quick peeked at us but didn't say nothing. I could tell she was scared. Me and Dory turned and run out the back door as fast as we could. We didn't stop running 'til we was halfway to the river.

It was no fun being at the river like before. We hid ourselves in a bunch of bushes and set there, silent, afraid to move. We didn't have no breakfast, and by the time the sun was high, we was starving. A few people come past in canoes, but they never seen us. When the sun got low, and our stomachs was screaming for food, and our mouths was dry as a bone, we crawled out of the bushes and headed back to Aunt Mary's. We walked slow even though we was thirsty and hungry: scared of what might be waiting for us back at the house.

When we got close to the house, we hid behind some bushes so Pa couldn't see us if he was there. I peeked through the leaves for any sign of him but didn't see nothing. Dory was crouched down beside me, not making a sound. I put my hand on her shoulder and said, "I don't see no sign of him or his truck. Maybe he took off."

Dory looked up at me and said, "But he might come back. Then what?"

"We gotta get back to Aunt Mary. She'll know what to do. She'll help us get back home."

We got back up and started down the road. Our eyes was peeled to the house for any sign of Pa. As we got closer, we dodged in and out of whatever we could find to keep outta sight. When we got to the porch, we set down on the ground with our backs against the house, listening for what was going on inside. Nothing. The place was silent.

Dory was squeezing my arm real tight, and I said, "I don't hear nothing. I think he musta left."

"I don't hear nothing neither. But I'm scared to go in there. He might be waiting to surprise us or something."

An old dandelion digger was leaned up against the house next to the porch. I grabbed it and said, "I'll protect us. I ain't gonna let nothing happen to you. Stay right behind me. I'll go first." Waving the digger in front of me, I said, "I got this to protect us. If he's in there, and tries anything, I'll stab him with it."

I got up slow and could feel Dory grabbing tight to the top of my pants. I took a look through the window next to the door but didn't see nobody. I couldn't hear a sound coming from the house. The doorknob turned easy, and I pushed the door open a crack. Still no sound in the house. I pushed a little more, and the door give a squeak. Me and Dory froze in place and listened. Nothing. My heart was beating hard and fast, and I could feel the shudder in my body again.

Not hearing nothing, I got the door open enough for me and Dory to slip through. We stood inside the door for a bit, listening. All was quiet. With the digger stuck out in front of me, I whispered, "Come on. Stay close by me," and being as quiet as I could, took a step.

We inched through the living room, past the kitchen, and down the hall. I seen Aunt Mary's bedroom door was open, and I heard a sound like maybe she was napping and turned over in her sleep. I waved my hand for Dory to keep moving, and we stepped in front of the open door.

Aunt Mary was naked. Her face was red and bloody, and her hands and feet was tied to the bed so her legs was kept open. She wasn't moving, and it looked like she was passed out. Pa was on top of her having his way.

Dory let out a scream and I dropped the digger. Fear froze my legs in place. I couldn't move. Dory stood there shaking and crying.

Pa was up in a flash, naked as a new born chick, and charging at us. He hit me first and knocked me hard into Dory. We both smashed against the wall and landed on the floor. Before I could make a move, Pa grabbed me and Dory by our arms and dragged us into our bedroom. He ripped out the light cord and tied us to our beds like he done to Momma that time. Then slammed the door as he left.

I forgot all about being hungry and thirsty. Fear overtook me. Me and Dory didn't talk. We just laid there, shaking. As bad as he was, I couldn't believe my pa would do something like that—and to his sister. My hate for him grew bigger as I tried to figure out what he was gonna do to us.

Sometime, long after it turned dark, we musta fell asleep. Because the next thing I know, the sun's beating down on my face through the window.

Chapter Twenty-One

~~~~~~~~~~~~~~~~~~~~~~~~~~~~~~~~~~~

Me and Dory was both awake, but we laid there not saying nothing. My wrist was hurting from the cord Pa used to tie me down, and I peed the bed. I figured I'd be beat for sure. The door swung open and I closed my eyes tight, pretending to be asleep. The sound of shuffling feet come toward me, and the stink of B.O. reached me before Pa did. He untied me first, then Dory. We both stayed still, too scared to move.

Pa stopped at the door and said, "Get your asses up. Pack your stuff and get to the kitchen. We gotta get a move on."

It took a minute to get all our stuff rounded up and into the suitcase. When we got to the kitchen, Pa was setting at the table chugging a beer. He slammed the empty down and reached for another one. He musta been going at it for a while because there was two empties next to the one he just finished.

Aunt Mary was at the stove, barefoot, and wearing a slip with one strap broke. She didn't say nothing or look at us. She fixed four plates of eggs, buttered toast with jelly, and big glasses of orange juice.

When she put the plates on the table, I could see her eyes was red, she had a bruised cheek, and a split lip.

Me and Dory set down opposite Pa, and Aunt Mary set at the end of the table. Nobody said nothing the whole time we was eating. We was afraid to look up at Pa and kept staring down at our plates. I could've ate lots more, because the last food I had was dinner two days before. But I didn't say nothing for fear it might get Pa more riled up.

When we was finished, Aunt Mary got up, cleared off the table, and stood at the sink with her back to us. I'm sure she didn't want us to see her any more than we already had. Pa stood and said, "Go get your suitcase. We're leaving."

While we was in the bedroom getting the bag, I heard Pa growl at Aunt Mary, "You keep your mouth shut. One word out of you, and I know where to find you. And you don't want that. Trust me." I didn't hear nothing from Aunt Mary.

I walked out first carrying the suitcase with Dory right behind. Pa was waiting at the door. Aunt Mary was still standing at the sink and didn't say nothing as we walked out. I sneaked a quick peek at her but didn't say nothing neither. I wanted to go grab her and run outta there as fast as we could. But I knew we'd never make it past Pa. Tears filled my eyes when the door shut behind us. But I pinched 'em back because my Pa would beat a sissy boy. And boys that cried was sissy boys to him.

I don't remember much about the ride home. Me and Dory set in the truck looking straight ahead at the dashboard and the road. I set as still as the park statue, hoping Pa wouldn't pay attention to me if I was froze in place. We stopped at a market in the first town we come to, and Pa bought a quart of beer. He didn't get nothing for me and Dory. Nobody talked the whole way to the farm. The only sound other than Pa taking chugs from the bottle was the whine of the engine and *whoosh* of passing cars and trucks. About twenty minutes out of Hellridge, I had to go so bad I thought I was gonna poop myself. The pain got pretty fierce, but I kept pinching my cheeks together to keep from blowing. I figured *that* pain wasn't as bad as the pain Pa would give me if I asked him to stop.

Pa pulled into the drive at the farm and stopped before we got to the house. He grabbed me and Dory by our hair and jerked our heads up so his face was right in ours. Dory let out a whimper but cut it off real quick. I wanted to yell from the pain of my hair being ripped out, but I didn't. He give a hard tug on our hair and said, "Listen you little shits. You say anything to anybody about what you seen at Aunt Mary's, and you'll be sorry. One word, and you won't have a Momma no more. Got it?"

We just stared into his evil eyes. I couldn't make words come out. He pulled our faces closer to his and said, "Do you get it?" I bobbed my head a little, so he'd know I got it. He pushed our heads back into the seat and parked by the house.

Momma musta seen me and Dory was in the truck when we drove up because she was on the porch by the time we got out. "Why, what are you guys doing here? I was about ready to go meet you at the station."

Dory run up to Momma crying and threw her arms around her but didn't say nothing. I got the suitcase outta the truck and started for the house, looking at the ground the whole way. When I got near Momma, she dropped to her knees and pulled me and Dory into her, holding us tight and kissing the top of our heads.

"I missed you two so much. Why so sad looking? Didn't you have fun? What's wrong?"

I raised my head, tried not to cry, and with a shaky voice, said, "Nothing's wrong, Momma. We had a good time."

I could tell the way Momma looked at me she didn't believe me. She looked at Pa and said, "What's wrong with these two? What happened, Paul?"

The devil glared at us, boring holes through me and Dory. "Nothing!" That's all he said before getting back in the truck and driving off.

Momma watched him leave, and we went into the house. Dory wouldn't let go of Momma's dress. I wouldn't of neither, but I had to get to the bathroom before I made a mess all over.

When I come out of the bathroom, Momma was on the couch hugging Dory. She patted the cushion next to her for me to join 'em. I set and looked down at my knees. Momma pulled us into her and said, "What's wrong? Did your pa hurt you?"

Real quick, I said, "No."

"Did something happen at Aunt Mary's?"

I said, "No."

"Listen. You know you can talk to me about anything that's bothering you. I can tell by the way you're acting that something's wrong. Please, talk to me. Let me help you."

Me and Dory didn't say nothing. We started bawling and pressing into Momma. It felt so good to have her close. I wanted to tell her about what happened to Aunt Mary, but I was afraid of what Pa would do to her if he found out. I didn't want her to get hurt, or worse.

Momma let it go. When we stopped crying, she give us a kiss and said, "You can talk to me when you're ready. Would you like some lunch?"

Me and Dory both nodded that we would.

Momma went to the kitchen and made us tuna salad sandwiches with chips. Me and Dory set silent on the couch until Momma called us to the table. After we ate, me and Dory went to our bedrooms. I got in bed and pulled the covers up over my head. I squeezed my eyes shut to make the picture of Pa on Aunt Mary go away, but it didn't. I kept seeing the same picture over and over. I musta fell asleep, because the next thing I heard was Momma calling for dinner.

Momma didn't press us no more about what was wrong. I think she knew we was too scared to talk about it—whatever it was. We set on the porch that night and watched the moon come up. It was big and round and yellow. I wished I could get away to the moon with Momma and Dory and never come back. We was all still. The only sound was the crickets talking to each other. I wondered if cricket daddies was nice to their wife and kids.

Chapter Twenty-Two

~~~~~~~~~~~~~~~~~~~~~~~~~~~~~~~~~~~~~

Momma took me and Dory to work with her the day after we come home from Aunt Mary's. We didn't know where Pa took off to, or when he'd come back. I was glad not to be left in the house without Momma. Being alone with Pa always made me scared. I couldn't have stood it after what I seen him do to his sister.

I don't remember much about the walk to Steiner's that day. My mind was all foggy. The picture of Pa on Aunt Mary, and the look of horror on her face, kept going round and round in my head. Momma talked some and tried to sound like nothing was wrong. She asked us questions about our time at Aunt Mary's in a way so's not to upset us.

"Did you go to the market where Aunt Mary works?"

I said, "Yeah."

"Did she take you to the Frosty Drive In for ice cream?"

"Yeah." Dory didn't say nothing.

"What kind of ice cream did you get?"

"Chocolate shakes."

"Yum! That sounds so good. I haven't had a shake in forever. Did you have one too, Dory?"

Dory didn't say nothing. She just bobbed her head a bit. Momma didn't press it.

We walked quiet for a ways. The sound of gravel crunching under our feet was louder than I remembered from before. I never seen Dory look up once the whole way to town. Her eyes was staring down at the road. My eyes was pointed down most of the time too.

Momma asked us some more questions.

"Did you walk to the river by Aunt Mary's?"

I said, "Uh huh."

"Did you know your dad was coming to get you?"

"No."

"Was he there long?"

"No."

"What did you do while he was there?"

I didn't say nothing. Neither did Dory. I felt light in the head like I was gonna pass out. My feet kept moving without me doing anything to make 'em go. All of a sudden we was at Steiner's. It felt like we was at home—then snap—we was at the cafe.

Momma set us in a booth close to the kitchen door where she could keep an eye on us. I seen her talking to Mr. Steiner. He'd shake his head and look over to where we was setting.

Me and Dory didn't talk or even look at each other. After a bit, Mr. Steiner come over with two new coloring books and a big pile of crayons.

"Here you go guys. You look like you could use something to do."

I said, "Thanks," without looking up.

"You bet. Give me a holler if you need anything."

I didn't say nothing. Mr. Steiner disappeared back in the kitchen.

There was a pay phone in one corner of the cafe. I seen Momma go to it during her break and put in some money. She stood there for a second, then said, "Mary?" I didn't hear no more of the conversation. But I knew by the look on Momma's face when she got off the phone that Aunt Mary'd told what happened. She stood real still and put her hand on the wall like she was trying to keep from falling down. Her other hand was cupped over her mouth. She turned to the wall and I seen her shoulders shaking up and down. She cried silent like that for a long time.

Mr. Steiner come out of the kitchen and seen something was wrong with Momma. He hurried over to her and put a hand on her back. Momma turned to him and laid her head on his chest. Mr. Steiner just stood there holding her until she stopped crying. They talked for a while, and then Momma took off her apron and come over to where we was setting.

"Come on kids. We're going home."

Momma started walking to the door, so me and Dory jumped up to follow. She walked real fast and didn't say nothing. We had to run-walk to keep up with her.

The first thing Momma did when she got in the house was go to the fridge and pull out a beer. I never seen her do that before. She stood with her back to us and took a couple pulls on the bottle. Her hands was shaking when she set down at the kitchen table. She called us over and told us to set.

Her face was gray and her voice sounded dead, when she said, "Aunt Mary told me what happened." Tears come to her eyes and she took another drink of beer. "I'm so sorry you guys. You should never have had to see that. What your dad did is wrong. Terrible!" Then she put her head on the table and bawled.

I got up and put my arms around Momma. Dory did too. I was scared of what would happen to Momma and Aunt Mary if Pa found out Aunt Mary told.

I said, "Don't tell Pa you know. He's gonna hurt Aunt Mary if you do. And I know he'll do something bad to you and Dory too. He said we wouldn't have you no more if we told. Please Momma, don't say nothing."

We all started to cry and hold tight to each other. I guess we was making quite a racket, because the next thing I knew, the front door slammed shut. That knocked the crying out of us, and we jerked our heads to the sound.

There he was. The devil himself. Standing by the door with a six-pack in his hand and an evil look on his face.

Chapter Twenty-Three

~~~~~~~~~~~~~~~~~~~~~~~~~~~~~~~~~~~~~~

Momma jumped up from the table and flew across the room at Pa. She screamed, "You bastard!" and run right into him with her arms stretched out in front of her like the blade on a snowplow. She hit him with everything she had and knocked him back into the door. He landed on his butt, and beers was rolling all over the floor. Momma's arms kept whipping back and forth, and her fists smashed into Pa's face with every swing. Me and Dory stood looking with our eyes wide and mouths dropped open.

I thought for sure Momma was gonna kill him. But things changed as fast as they begun. Pa's arm drew back, and he smashed his fist hard into Momma's face. She went flying across the room and laid still when she landed. Pa crawled over and set on top of her. He started slugging her in the face as hard as he could, over and over.

I unfroze and run to Momma as fast as I could. I started beating on Pa but wasn't big enough to do no damage. Where was that spinach when I needed it?

Pa took a break from smacking Momma and smashed his fist into my face, sending me flying through the air. I remember hearing Dory let out a scream. Then everything went black.

When I come to, Dory was crying and screaming, "Stop! Stop! Stop! Mommy! Oh, Mommy!" And I heard a sound like a hammer banging into wood. But it wasn't no hammer. It was my Momma's head being beat into the floor.

I opened my eyes as best I could but didn't have no strength to get up. My sight was blurry, but I could tell Pa was still on Momma. The sound of Momma's head hitting the floor finally stopped. I seen Pa set there looking at her with his face all twisted up. Then he spit on her. Momma's face was bloody, and a red pool was gathering around her head. She didn't move. My momma was dead: just like Pa said she'd be if we told. But we didn't. Aunt Mary did.

I looked over at Dory. Her whole body was shaking, and the floor was wet where she stood. Pa run over, grabbed her arm, and jerked her over to where I was. He pushed her down on the floor next to me. Pa went over to Momma and stared down at her for a long time. Then he turned to us and said, "Giddup! Giddup and help me."

Me and Dory didn't move. Pa come to us and yanked us up by our arms. He dragged us through the house and out the back door to the tool shed. He pulled out two shovels and told us to dig a hole by the side of the shed. I never been so scared in my life. I figured me and Dory'd be dead if we didn't do what he asked. Dory wasn't strong enough to do much, but she did her best. I was bigger, so I had to do most of the work. There was no sound except shovels hitting dirt.

The hole wasn't very deep: maybe two foot. Pa snatched the shovels when the hole was to his liking and tossed 'em on the ground. Me and Dory was tired, dirty, and scared. We stood there like zombies.

Pa said to follow him and headed to the house. He come back when we didn't move and grabbed our hair. It hurt so bad, but he drug us all the way to where Momma was. She hadn't moved since I last seen her. The blood around her head looked like it was starting to set. I knew she was gone and wished I could be there with her.

"You each take a leg and help me get her out back."

I couldn't make my legs work. I don't think Dory could neither. But a hard knock to our heads got us moving. Pa took Momma's hands and started to pull. Me and Dory each held a leg. I couldn't look at Momma. Everything wasa fog around me. I slipped on something, and when I looked down, there was red stuff on my shoe. I didn't wanna think about what it was.

The next thing I knew, we was at the hole. Pa dropped Momma's arms and said,

"Roll her in."

It was the weirdest thing: it was daytime, but I know I heard a owl hooting somewhere off in the distance. I stood and listened until a slap upside my head brung me back from the owl. I couldn't really feel nothing, not even the slap. Everything around me was fuzzy except a little spot right in front of my eyes. It was like I was dead. My mind was shut off. I musta pushed. I think Dory did too. I don't remember seeing nothing, but a thud told me Momma was in the hole.

Pa give us the shovels and said, "Fill it."

No tears come to my eyes. I just stayed on my knees, trying not to look down. When I told Doc Samuelson about it later, he said it was because I was in shock: that people can only take so much bad stuff before they turn off; like soldiers that seen too much killing.

The hole got filled, but I'm not sure who done it. I have a picture in the back of my head of me holding a shovel full of dirt, so I musta helped. I remember Pa throwing the shovels down and pushing me and Dory over to the shed. He shoved us to the floor without saying nothing. The shock of hitting the floor brung me outta the fog a bit, and my eyes cleared some. Then the door slammed shut, and I heard the latch slide into place. It was pitch black except for a little light that come in under the door. We was trapped.

When my sight got used to the dark, I could see Dory setting next to me, shaking. I put my arm around her, and she started to bawl. We clung to each other while the thought of what we just done took hold. No words was spoke.

It wasn't no time before I heard Pa's truck start up and tear off outta the yard. I knew where he was heading. But I didn't have no way to warn Aunt Mary.

Chapter Twenty-Four

~~~~~~~~~~~~~~~~~~~~~~~~~~~~~~~~~~~~~

The shed fell silent after the roar of Pa's truck died out: except for the quiet sobs coming from Dory. We set there on the floor for a long time; my arm pulling Dory close; her head leaning on my shoulder. The picture of Momma's head slamming into the floor, and the sound of her body hitting the hole, kept going round and round in my head. My brain felt like it was gonna blow.

After a while, my butt went numb from setting so long on the hard floor. When I stood up, the shed started to spin, and I thought I was gonna keel over. I put my foot out to keep from falling. Dory didn't get up. She laid down on her side and pulled her knees up to her chest: like I seen a little baby do before.

There was a light bulb hanging from the ceiling of the shed with a string to pull to turn it on. I remembered it from the first time me and Dory went exploring. It was too dark to see the string, but I had a good idea where it was. I used the light coming in from under the door and moved to the middle of the shed. I swung my arms around above my head, hoping to find the string. It musta been high up because all I hit was cobwebs and air.

An old wood box set on the floor next to the door. I drug it to the place where I thought the light should be and stood on it. The string was easy to grab, and I give it a tug. The light come on all right, but it was a little bulb and not very bright. At least we could see what was around us, so we knew nothing was hiding in the corner to snatch us. I guess that helped a little. But not much.

I don't know why I wasn't crying. Dory cried for a long time before she finally stopped and went silent. Maybe my hate for my pa overtook the sad. I got off the box and set on the floor with my back against the wall. As scared as I was, my nine-year-old brain kept thinking of ways to get my pa and keep me and Dory alive. I figured he'd come back to kill us once he was done with Aunt Mary.

My mind was whirring when I seen a shadow creep across the light coming under the door. My heart about jumped outta my chest, and I couldn't breathe. The shadow moved real slow from one side of the crack to the other. It moved a bit, then stopped, then moved again. I knew it was my pa. Just when I started feeling dizzy, I heard the flap of wings and the caw from a crow as it took off outside the shed. I sucked in a big breath and leaned back against the wall. It was awhile before my heart beat normal again. Dory kept breathing steady, but she didn't move or say nothing.

Sleep musta overtook me, because the next thing I remember is opening my eyes and seeing the light under the door was dimmer, and the shed wasn't so hot. Thoughts of Momma slammed into my head. I felt like I was gonna hurl. "Dory." No answer. "Dory, are you awake?" Still no answer.

My stomach finally settled, but my body was stiff and sore from setting so long. I got up, stretched, and started walking back and forth from one side of the shed to the other, trying not to think about what happened earlier. My eye caught what looked like a jar of something setting on the shelf. It turned out to be a jar of red beets Grandma musta canned. It was covered with dust and spider webs. I didn't see no spiders, so I pulled it off the shelf. The lid was rusty and held down with a metal clamp. I tried to pop the lid, but it didn't budge. The clamp eventually broke with the help of a rusty, old screwdriver. "Dory, I found a jar of beets. You want some?" Nothing. Just steady breathing. I wasn't really hungry, but I set on the floor, kinda dazed, and popped beets in my mouth. It was something to do.

The light under the door got less and less: then it was gone. Fear grabbed me hard when I seen it was night. Pa could come back at any time. Dory hadn't moved or spoke since she laid on the floor. I felt all alone but knew I had to do something to try and protect us. Then I remembered the ax I seen hanging above the work bench the day me and Dory first looked in the shed.

It felt heavy when I pulled it off the nails. The handle was covered with dust, and the head was rusty: like everything else in the shed. But it felt like maybe we had a chance. I started swinging at the door, but it wasn't no use. The shed was made of heavy metal, and alls I did was put little dents in it. The loud banging didn't stir Dory.

I set back down with the ax out in front of me and one hand gripping the handle. Fear and hate took turns running around in my head. Pictures of Momma flashed in and out of focus. I wanted to cry but couldn't. I don't know how long I set there before I heard the pickup pull down the drive. Pins started sticking my face, and it was hard to breathe. I had to do something, and fast. But what?

"Dory wake up! Pa's back! Get up! Hurry!" She still never moved. It was like she was in another world only she knew about.

I jumped back up on the box and pulled the light string. Everything went black. I stood silent, listening for any little sound. It wasn't no time before I heard heavy footsteps coming toward the shed. I moved real quiet over to the side of the door and raised the ax above my head. Panic caused my whole body to shake, and the heavy ax almost made my arms give out. But I stood there, waiting. I didn't know what else to do. If I didn't do nothing, we was dead meat for sure.

The footsteps come closer and stopped outside the door. I squeezed hard to the ax handle and held my breath. Nothing happened. Then the latched squeaked open. I squeezed the handle so hard I thought it was gonna snap. The door swung open and a strip of moonlight cut thorough the shed and shined on Dory. I caught a whiff of B.O. and booze and knew for sure it was Pa.

"Come out you little shits. I wanna talk to you." Silence. "I said get your asses out here." More silence.

Not hearing nothing, or seeing me, he took a step into the shed. The second I seen his head come through the door, I brung the ax down as hard as I could. It struck him on the side of the head with a dull thud. He just stood there: not coming in or going out. Just when I thought I didn't do no damage, his head turned to me with the ax still stuck in, and he fell to the shed floor.

I was froze in place. He landed smack in front of Dory with his dead eyes staring right at her. That brung Dory out of her daze and she let out a scream. I grabbed her arm, pulled her to her feet, and said, "Let's get outta here." We run out the door as fast as we could go with Dory scream-crying at the top of her lungs. We run down the drive to the road and turned toward town.

I don't know how long we run, or how far. My mind is missing a bunch of what happened after we hit the road. The next thing I remember is flashing lights from a cop car, and Dory standing next to me. The town cop was knelt down in front of us with one hand holding my arm and the other holding Dory's. He kept asking, "Are you hurt? What happened? Where's your Momma?" And them lights kept flashing. Neither of us said nothing. We was wore out from running, and the shock had set in. I think the cop thought I was hurt because of all the beet juice on me and the splatter from Pa.

The cop put us in the back of his car and shut the door. I figured I was gonna go to jail for killing my pa, but I didn't care. He was a bad man who wasn't never gonna hurt nobody again. The ride to town is missing from my mind. The next thing I knew, we was in the cop station.

Chapter Twenty-Five

~~~~~~~~~~~~~~~~~~~~~~~~~~~~~~~~~~~~

The lights was bright, voices come at me from everywhere at once, and everything looked fuzzy. That's what I remember about going into the cop station. I don't know how I made it in. But boom, there I was.

Me and Dory was put in a little room that had some chairs and a table. A lady cop and the cop that brung us in set on the other side of the table and asked us questions. I knew they was talking, but I couldn't piece together what they was saying. My mind wouldn't focus. The words come at me without sentences: "Pa . . . happened . . . what . . . your momma . . . running." My mind was like a big, empty barn with words bouncing off the walls that I couldn't make no sense of. My mouth couldn't get words out, so I just set, quiet.

There was a spider crawling up the wall behind the cops that caught my eye. Staring at it helped me block everything else out. I wanted to snap my fingers and turn into a spider. Free. Away from people, the lights, the noise: with nothing to think about but building a web in a dark corner and waiting for my next meal.

Somebody brought hamburgers to us

while the words banged around my head. Leastways, I think they did. My mind has a memory of smelling hamburgers, but not of eating 'em.

The questions stopped when they realized we was in too much shock to answer. Dory set there silent for a long time, then got up, walked to the corner, laid down, and curled up like a baby again. That took my mind off the spider. The lady cop got a blanket and put it over Dory. Then she set down next to her and rubbed her back. The cops treated us real good.

I don't know how long we was at the station before a man and woman come to get us. They give us clean underpants, a dress for Dory, and long pants and a T-shirt for me. We musta been pretty dirty, and my clothes was covered with beet juice and Pa's blood. I was glad to get out of 'em.

It was starting to get light when they took us out of the station to the car. The man carried Dory and held my hand. The lady helped me and Dory get in the back seat, then set in the middle with me on one side and Dory on the other. She put her arms around us and pulled us into her. It felt soft and good. The man got in and drove.

Nobody said nothing as we went down the highway. The hum of the engine and slap of the tires was the only sound. My head felt nice pressed into the lady, but not like with Momma. I pushed that thought outta my head because I knew I was never gonna lay against Momma again. I felt like crying, but there wasn't no tears.

We passed by the spot where Grandpa and Grandma was killed, and I got a whiff of flowers. It musta been the lady's perfume. I knew we was close to the farm, so I turned my eyes down from the window. But as I did, I caught a glimpse of flashing red and blue lights off in the distance and wondered if they'd found Momma. How was she? Maybe she wasn't dead. Maybe they got there in time and saved her. Maybe I'd see her again. But no, there was too much blood. A shiver went through me, and a silent tear run down my face. The lady pulled me closer.

The sun was up when the car turned into the driveway at Willow Bend State Hospital. The hospital is about a hundred miles from Hellridge and was named after the nearby town. It's where South Dakota keeps its crazies.

What I first seen looked nice: there was lots of trees, a big yard with a fountain in the middle, and benches scattered around. But I got a fright when the building come into view. It was the biggest one I ever seen. The front was made outta stone blocks the color of dry dirt, and there was bars across the windows. A tower rose high above the entrance and looked like a place where folks might be locked up. I remembered seeing one kinda like it in a storybook Momma read to us about a girl with long hair that was kept in a tower. I think a prince come to save her. But I didn't believe no prince lived around Willow Bend.

I crossed my fingers that we wasn't going in, but it didn't work. The motor shut off and the man got out. He opened the back door and helped us out. The lady picked Dory up, the man took my hand, and we started walking to the front door. My heart was banging, and I thought about turning around to make a run for it. But I figured I wouldn't get too far. Besides, where was I gonna go? And what about Dory?

A pretty lady wearing a yellow dress and a big smile was waiting for us at the door. She shook hands with the man and lady, then said, "You must be Dory, and you young man, must be Jake. Welcome to Willow Bend. We're so happy you came. I think you're going to like it here." Miss Wilkerson was her name, and she still runs the place.

Miss Wilkerson took us down a long hall and into a room she said was for me and Dory. There was two beds, two dressers for our stuff, and a desk and chair for each of us. It was painted a nice green color, and there was some posters on the walls. Then my eye caught the bars on the windows, and I said, "What's them bars for?"

"Oh, don't you worry about those.

They're there to help keep everyone safe. Come on, let's go meet some of the other kids."

A flash hit me of Momma lying on the floor, her face smashed and covered with blood. My arms went dead and pins stabbed my face.

When I come to, it was dark outside, and I was curled up on the bed like Dory. I started seeing Momma staring at me, her mouth moving like she was trying to talk, blood running out her eyes. I seen Pa's head with the ax sticking out. I heard Dory screaming, the sound of shovels scraping dirt, the thud of Momma's body when she dropped in the hole. I rocked back and forth, back and forth, back and forth. Then it was light out.

People—nurses I think—come in our room with food, tried to feed us, and left. Sometimes I ate a little, sometimes I didn't. They tried to talk to us, but I never heard Dory say nothing, and I didn't neither. Once a week or so, a big lady wearing a white uniform come in and give us clean sheets. She never said nothing. I was glad. When the people was gone and the room was quiet, I laid in my bed and rocked back and forth, back and forth, back and forth. It give me some comfort and helped take away the pictures and sounds that run over and over again in my head. Dory never moved unless they come in and rolled her over: which they done several times every day.

They took me down to see Doc Richards—the hospital shrink—a couple times a week. Dory seen him too, but not at the same time as me. At first, I never said nothing to him. But after a while I started talking: a little at first; then more as time passed. The worst part was talking about the day Momma died and I killed Pa. The doc never pushed me though, and we stopped talking about it as soon as I started shaking.

After seeing the doc for a few weeks, I didn't stay in bed so much: I'd stand staring out the window at people in the yard, look through books the nurse brung, and eat at my desk. Doc Richards said it would be good for me to spend time with some of the other kids, but I didn't want nothing to do with 'em. Being with Dory was fine. I was used to her. But it made me nervous thinking about talking with others, or worse yet, having 'em touch me.

The time with Doc Richards didn't seem to do much for Dory. She got so she'd turn herself in bed, but she didn't get up or talk. I tried talking to her some, but she laid silent with her eyes locked on some far-off place.

One day, about six months in, Dory was moved to another part of the hospital. I begged 'em to leave her be. I told 'em I would help her get better, that she needed me, that she'd die if we was apart. But it didn't do no good—Dory was gone. I cried the whole day and didn't eat nothing. After that, I only seen her a couple times a week.

A boy was moved in with me a month after Dory left. I hated him at first for making Dory move and didn't talk to him for a long time. He became part of the room after a while, and it wasn't so bad having someone to talk to. But he was the only one. I never did get friendly with the other kids.

My life at the hospital for eleven years was pretty much the same: eat, sleep, stare out the window, talk to Doc, and take meds. I never had a visitor the whole time.

I left Willow Bend the day I turned twenty. I still had bad dreams, seen stuff in my head that made me shake, and didn't want nobody to touch me. But Doc said I was better, and if I seen the doc he referred me to—Doc Samuelson—I'd get even better over time.

When I went to say goodbye, Dory was setting in a wheelchair with her eyes fixed out the window. She was eighteen but looked a lot older. She had dark circles around her eyes, and her short, chopped-off hair had streaks of gray in it. I knelt down beside her and said, "Dory, it's me, Jake." No response. "Dory, I come to tell you I'm leaving today. I'm not gonna be able to see you so much. But I will come to visit as much as I can. And when you're outta here, you can come live with me. We'll be together like before. Promise." Still nothing. I bent over, give her a kiss on the forehead, and walked away. I stopped at the door and said, "I love you Dory. Take care." I cried as I walked down the hall, away from my sister, the only living kin I knew of.

The sun was shining when I walked out the front door. The same door I walked through eleven years before: a scrawny, scared, nine-year-old killer. I was happy, sad, and scared to be leaving: happy to be starting a new life, sad to be leaving my sister behind, and scared that I wouldn't make it.

The Willow Bend van was waiting. Ben, the driver, give me a wave. I climbed in the back and watched out the window as the dirt-colored tower faded in the distance. Next stop—Hellridge.

Chapter Twenty-Six

~~~~~~~~~~~~~~~~~~~~~~~~~~~~~~~~~~

It's been three years since I moved outta Willow Bend and into Grandpa Earl and Grandma Thelma's old house. The place looks pretty much like when I was a kid living in the trailer out back. The trailer's gone: Momma sold it after they died to help with expenses. But other than a coat of paint, which I done myself, it's the same.

Bob, my boss and manager of the Melody Bowl, give me a job washing dishes two days after I got back. My shift runs five o'clock to nine o'clock every night, seven days a week, more if he needs me. It's minimum wage, but enough to keep me going since my expenses ain't much. The dishwasher sets back in a corner of the kitchen away from where the fry cook works. It's perfect because I don't have to talk to no one. Plastic baskets for the burgers and fries, glasses from the bar, and silverware is all there is to wash.

Three months ago, I started working a few hours a week at Brannigan's Garage: training really. It's an auto repair shop here in Hellridge where Grandpa Earl always brung his car. I remember him saying it was the best shop in town. Old man Brannigan told me he wants to retire someday and asked if I'd like to take over. I figure mechanic work pays better than washing dishes, and so far I like it. Maybe I could turn it into a career.

Doc Samuelson's office is about two blocks from the bowling alley, so I meet with him once a month before my Wednesday shift. He helps me a lot with the bad things that still come in my mind sometimes. Spending more time with people is the thing he says will help me the most. I try, and I believe it's working. I'm talking more with Bob and the fry cook, and I even talked with customers at Brannigan's a couple times. I told Doc I wanted to get off my meds some day and asked him what he thought. He thinks that'll happen, just not yet.

The Greyhound makes a stop in Willow Bend, and I catch it every few months when I get a day off work. It's both a happy and sad trip: I'm happy to be with Dory, but sad to see how she is. She mostly sits in her wheelchair by the window when she's not in bed. She doesn't say nothing, but sometimes makes a humming sound. A couple times she turned her eyes to me when I said her name. I guess that's something. Maybe she'll get well some day and come live with me. I hope so.

I ride my bike to the cemetery every week to visit Momma and tend to her grave:

pull weeds and keep the headstone clean. I miss her so much. Things I don't talk about to nobody, I tell to Momma. I know she can hear me. It would be so good to hear her voice again. She always had a way to make me feel peaceful.

I don't know where my pa's buried, or even if he's buried. Maybe they just burned him up and let his ashes blow away. I don't know and I don't care. I never asked and I don't plan to. I'm just glad he ain't around no more to cause hurt to me and Dory. He already done way too much of that. If there is a hell, I hope he's there suffering the same pain he give to us all them years.

My friend Dorothy's regular visits are helping me get over the fear of being around folks. We give each other a quick hug now every time she leaves, and I don't tense up like I did the first time she done it. She's been telling me about her niece in Colorado, says she's my age, super smart, and a good person. Dorothy invited her to come for a visit and wants me to meet her. I'm not sure if I'm ready for that yet. I guess we'll see what happens when she gets here.

Yesterday, I rode out to our old farm. The closer I got, the more my stomach hurt and the sweatier my hands got. I almost turned around and went home, but I wanted to see if I could do it. I stopped by the mail box, the same one where I got beat up all them years ago, and a rush of memories almost knocked me off my bike, but I didn't run. Some of the trees had been cut down, so the house was visible. A young man and woman set on the porch where me and Dory used to set. They reminded me of Momma and my pa. Two little kids was running around the yard kicking a ball, screaming and laughing. The man give me a wave, and I give one back. They all looked so happy. I hoped they was.

It was good to see that peace had come to the farm: that a normal family lived there. The place deserved it after all the pain it seen.

Peddling back to town, my stomach eased and my hands dried. I done it. I went back to face the hell that was and didn't come apart. For the first time in a long time, a smile crossed my mouth, and I knew I was gonna make it.

Free Copy Of The Visitor

Visit www.stephenrossauthor.com for a FREE copy of my suspense/thriller short story "THE VISITOR" and Notice of New Books/Sales

~The Visitor Synopsis~

The morning broke like every other in the small Midwestern town of Porterville: quiet and peaceful. It's a farming community where church basement potlucks and Sunday drives in the country are the main sources of entertainment. Nothing much ever happened there until the arrival of the visitor.

Eighty-six-year-old resident Ima Plummer could not have imagined how her day would end when she awoke that fateful Wednesday.

You won't want to stop reading.

About The Author

Stephen Ross practiced law until retiring in 2017. His first novella, MEMOIR FROM HELL, received the 2019 Reader Views Reviewers Choice Award and the 2019 Independent Author Network Book of the Year Finalist Award. It was praised by Reader Views as "realistic and genuine … the ending is dramatic and haunting," and by author Anthony Avina as "an emotionally charged novel that needs to be read." Stephen's other work includes, POWER LUST, a legal and political thriller set in California, and a supernatural thriller, THE VISITOR. Born in Iowa and raised in Nebraska, Stephen now lives in San Diego, California. When he's not writing, he enjoys reading, hiking, camping, and movies. He can be reached via his website at www.stephenrossauthor.com on Facebook at www.facebook.com/stephenrosswriter, on LinkedIn at www.linkedin.com/in/stephen-ross-639114105, and on Twitter at www.twitter.com/stephenross48.

Also By Stephen Ross

<u>Novels</u>:
Power Lust

<u>Short Stories</u>:
The Visitor